Four Exciting Novels Every Month

Romance, conflict, danger and
faraway places...
All adding up to
the very special allure of

Mystique Books

You will be intrigued by the excitement
of exotic lands...

You will be thrilled by the beauty
of pure romance...

You will be gripped by the danger
of sinister schemes...

You will discover a whole new world!

Available wherever paperback books are sold.

What readers say about Mystique Books...

Sardinia was a perfect refuge...

Castel Terralba was grim and foreboding outside, but warm and welcoming within. Marion felt completely at ease for the first time in many months.

But she had yet to meet the castle's master, the proud, overbearing Don Carlo de Terralba. What she'd heard of him both intrigued and frightened her.

Marion expected him to be imperious and cruel. She knew his power was absolute.

Then there was a sharp rap on her bedroom door...the moment of truth had come.

Other

MYSTIQUE BOOKS

by MAGALI

For a free catalogue listing all available Mystique Books,
send your name and address to:

MYSTIQUE READER SERVICE,
M.P.O. Box 707, Niagara Falls, N.Y. 14302
In Canada: 649 Ontario St., Stratford, Ontario N5A 6W2

Vanishing Bride

by MAGALI

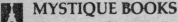

MYSTIQUE BOOKS

TORONTO・LONDON・NEW YORK
HAMBURG・AMSTERDAM・STOCKHOLM

VANISHING BRIDE/first published August 1977

Second printing October 1977
Third printing November 1977
Fourth printing December 1977
Fifth printing March 1978
Sixth printing July 1978
Seventh printing December 1978
Eighth printing December 1978
Ninth printing January 1979
Tenth printing May 1979
Eleventh printing July 1979
Twelfth printing August 1979
Thirteenth printing February 1980

ISBN 0-373-50001-7

PRINTED IN CANADA.

CHAPTER 1

The September roses were opening in the early-morning light as Marion locked the wrought-iron gates and cast a farewell glance past the garden and the terrace to the sea beyond. The water looked bluer and more brilliant than it had during the entire holiday—or perhaps she just thought it did, because she was leaving.

The lounge chairs, still warm from the blissful, dozing afternoons, were folded away; the games table was safely tucked inside and the hammock rolled up. She had put the masks and snorkel tubes in the cupboard until next year. The voices—calling, laughing, singing—were silent, the tennis balls still. The summer and its joys were over.

At least she had had ten more days than poor Stanni, called back so unexpectedly to an important business meeting. Now she, too, was leaving; and the pine-scented silence, heavy with rosemary and lavender, would settle undisturbed over the patios, the vines and olives on the hillside and the roofs of rosy tile. She hated saying goodbye. Always she felt a pang when she left l'Oursinade, as though her pretty little villa somehow knew its owner was deserting it.

She sighed, loaded the last of the suitcases into the trunk and began the half-hour drive to the station at Nice. She was reluctant to drive a small car all the way to Paris at this time of year, with so many lunatics on the road. It could go by the train-ferry and she would catch the ten o'clock plane.

But the holiday was not quite over. Until she was away from the coastline, with its beaches and pine woods and end-of-the-season visitors, she remained under their spell; she was still in the south of France.

As she drove, she considered the past few weeks and Stanni's departure. Poor darling, always having to give things up. Really, husbands led very demanding lives. She had so looked forward to driving back in the Mercedes, just the two of them, and now he'd had to go alone.

Why couldn't that wretched man in Brussels have waited another ten days to air his marketing problems and visit every store he owned in Flanders? That drive together from l'Oursinade to Paris would have meant so much to both of them, for it would have given them a chance to talk at length. Stanni worried her and she felt, somehow, that she was to blame.

With the motor purring softly as she wove adroitly through the traffic, her thoughts were fixed on the last stay at the summer place. It hadn't been an unqualified success, so far as sorting things out with Stanni went.

The women's pages were always full of marvelous advice on how to be a companion to your husband during vacation. In the relaxed atmosphere he would be open and you were supposed to grow close. Well, she had tried, but it hadn't quite worked. Stanni was forever water-skiing, or fishing or taking solo rides in the little speedboat. And he wasn't communicative at the best of times; rather an unsociable person, really, and so reserved he frightened her.

After nearly two years she still could not understand him. He put an enormous amount of energy into his work and always arrived home exhausted, too worn out to bother with her. Yet he was very charming; he remembered their anniversaries and special occasions, and he let her do exactly as she liked. That was it, perhaps. The ties were not strong enough. Marriage was rather different from what she had expected.

Modern city life does not make marriage very easy; time-consuming travel and the urban business world conspire to leave wives on their own a great deal. Stanni, with his head office in southeast Paris near the Porte d'Italie, could not very well drive all the way home for lunch every day: their home in la Celle Saint-Cloud was on the other side of the city.

"If we lived in town it would make no difference," he had said, when they were deciding to buy the house. "We could be up in Montmartre or down on the Champs Elysées, but I couldn't spend any more time at home. So let's be somewhere pleasant, away from the traffic and pollution."

Marion had coped with the solitude fairly well in the beginning. In a way she even welcomed it, for she was still grieving for her father, whose death had hastened her marriage. And then, of course, she told herself, there'll be the babies.

. Children were her dearest wish. She would have liked them as soon as possible and yearned over gossamer cradles in maternity store windows. But Stanni seemed to be in no great hurry.

"You're young," he had said, "you're only twenty-two, and I'm thirty. Why rush to meet responsibility? We can wait."

"But isn't that what marriage means?" she had asked.

"Certainly it is. But if we had a child now, well, I'm never home, I would hardly ever see it. Wait until I've got the business organized. Your father left problems, you know. I have to solve them. Still, it shouldn't be long now. We'll soon be seeing more of one another."

Darling Stanni, so conscientious, so determined to do the right thing. She was selfish to think of her needs so much, to harbor this obscure resentment. She must try to look at the situation from his point of view.

Nevertheless, she craved children desperately and had planned to talk to him about it during their holiday in the south. But the days were filled with friends and parties, tennis and sailing and fishing; she had allowed herself to be swept up in it all and somehow the moment never came. It was frustrating, disappointing.

REACHING NICE on schedule she filled out the necessary forms and handed over the car to be put on the train, then took a taxi to the airport. She was at the airline counter by nine-thirty.

"Any luggage?" enquired the ticket agent, as she tore out the duplicate on the ticket.

"Only this bag."

It was the usual blue canvas affair, the Air France flight bag that everybody carries. The woman gave her a boarding pass and told her the plane left at ten. Pass in hand Marion moved toward the departure lounge.

The woman ahead was a vision of elegance in a white suit, large green hat and matching shoes. They went through the gate together, each carrying her boarding pass carefully. Seeing an empty bench the two women sat down, their standard Air France bags on the floor in front of them. Similar bags were scattered all over the lounge.

An impersonal voice over the public address system announced a delay in flight 915 to Paris.

"Not mine," said the vision, with a friendly smile.

"Nor mine," Marion rejoined. "I'm on flight 458."

The other consulted her card. "458? Oh, me too." She glanced at her watch and added anxiously, "I hope that doesn't mean we'll be late as well."

"It might. They put on all these extra flights for people going home after the holidays; I suppose the timetables get upset."

"I think I'll go and ask."

She went to the information desk while Marion walked over to the glass doors and looked at the bustling scene outside. Various aircraft were being readied for takeoff; gangways were wheeled into place; crowded mini-buses darted out to the farthest runways; cases were piled high on luggage trucks.

"We're all right so far," her fellow traveler said as they sat on their bench again, and as though to confirm this news the loudspeaker invited passengers awaiting flight 458 to proceed to Gate A for immediate embarkation.

"Oh, look, we're right in front of it!" cried the woman in white. She grabbed her bag and ran to join the first wave through Gate A.

Heavens, she's in a hurry, thought Marion, amused. She collected the light coat she had left on the seat and slipped it on before sauntering between the double barriers that formed a sort of corridor to the exit gate.

Three children came pushing through, holding hands, and the whole family, mother and father included, surged past her as she was forced to make room. When the youngest dropped a parcel, he watched it roll away with such anguish that Marion went to the rescue, pursued it and returned it to him over the heads of yet another couple who had moved ahead of her in the line. By now she was one of the last.

A young woman took her card, tore off one section and handed it back. The passengers poured through the different doors and hastened to their respective aircraft. The elegant green hat was nowhere to be seen; doubtless its owner was already on board, safely ensconced in a seat by the window.

A stewardess stood at the foot of the ramp to the plane. Marion presented her boarding pass.

"Is this my flight?" she enquired.

"No. That one over there—that's 458."

A little farther on and somewhat out of breath, she reached the correct ramp, where a dark-complexioned man with a dazzling smile stood aside for her, murmuring something polite in a husky voice. She caught the word, "Señorita." *How nice and gallant Spaniards are,* she thought.

The stewardess waited, with her ladylike charm and regulation smile.

"Good morning, Madame. Good morning, Monsieur. You're the last on. We were about to close the doors."

The aircraft was packed. Marion fought and wriggled her way past people struggling to put their coats on the luggage racks overhead, until she reached the one vacant seat remaining. The engines started up and the plane began to move. From the P.A. system came the ritual announcement: "Place your hand luggage under your seats, please, and fasten your safety belts. You are asked not to smoke during takeoff. Thank you."

Worn out, Marion leaned back as the instructions were repeated in English. After staying awake half the night for fear of sleeping through the alarm she had been up at an unearthly hour, putting everything in order before shutting up the house for the winter. Then the drive and seeing to the car and the rush to reach the airport on time had left her quite exhausted. She dozed, lulled by the engines and the motion as the plane raced across the ground. When the stewardess appeared with some candy she took a piece automatically, without really waking up. With a great roar, they left the run-

way and rose into the air. Too far from the window to
see out, Marion surfaced briefly, then relapsed into
torpor.

The great engines, having performed the lift-off, re-
sumed their normal rhythm. The roaring died down
and as in a dream she half heard someone saying,
"Mesdames et Messieurs, Captain de Tourbet wel-
comes you aboard...." The words drifted away into
the clouds. Odd phrases came like misty gibberish.
"... cruising-speed will be ... we are flying over...."
But none of it made sense. It belonged to some cotton-
wool universe, over an empty void. Deliberately she
blocked the outside world and drifted into sleep, aware
of nothing but pinewoods, sand and sailboats; of a man
who skied effortlessly across water, of the beat of an
outboard motor.... Then a hand touched her shoulder.

"Yes? What is it?"

"Your tray, Madame."

Still hazy, she opened her eyes.

"Will you straighten your seat, please," the stewardess insisted.

Mechanically, Marion obeyed, noticing as she did so
that her neighbor was busily devouring chicken in as-
pic. She wasn't expecting such an enormous snack. The
stewardess released the folding table and behind her a
steward advanced with a tray of drinks.

"What will you have to drink Madame? Wine?
Beer?"

At this hour, she thought. *They must be crazy.*

"Water for me, thank you."

It might, of course, be some special holiday service,
but nothing of this sort had ever happened before on
the two hour's flight from Nice to Paris. She consulted
her watch. Eleven-thirty. That was odd; either the
plane was late, or her watch was wrong. Had she perhaps forgotten to wind it in her hurry to leave?

"Are we behind time?" she asked, when they came to collect the tray.

"No," replied one of the women, seizing it and dashing off.

As she spoke, the speaker overhead gave its stupefying answer to the question. "Mesdames et Messieurs," it announced, "in fifteen minutes we shall be landing at Málaga airport.

In a panic Marion turned to the man in the next seat. "Is this plane going to Málaga?"

"*Por favor?*" He looked at her blankly.

Desperately, she clutched the stewardess by the elbow. "Am I in a plane for Málaga?"

"Where did you think you were, Madame?"

"Paris. I got on, just now, at Nice."

"You're mistaken, Madame," said the woman, as though nothing ever surprised her. "We'll be in Málaga in a few minutes." Then, with sudden misgiving, "Didn't you hear the announcements?"

"I was asleep, I'm afraid," Marion admitted.

By now the hostess was definitely suspicious.

"I'll be right back. Have your ticket ready, please."

Her hand shaking a little in consternation, Marion took her flight bag from under the seat; she opened it, and consternation turned to panic. As though in a nightmare, she could recognize no single object in it. There was a vanity case with a lipstick and powder compact; a lizard skin purse and a matching wallet bulging with money; a bunch of keys, including what appeared to be suitcase keys; an envelope addressed to somebody called Florence Montagne, whose identity card with photograph attached was there, too, in a holder. She had seen that face before, but who? Where? Then all at once it dawned on her. This bag belonged to the woman in the airport at Nice. They had both stood up, she remembered, and when they sat down again must have changed places without noticing. When the

other woman ran so fast, she had taken the wrong
flight bag. They all looked alike, so Marion, in her turn,
had merely picked up the one at her feet. Sure enough,
she found a Nice-Paris ticket with the flight number
458 and the holder's name. The Stewardess reappeared
as she examined it.

"May I see your ticket, Madame?"

"Yes. But I—"

Her explanation was cut short, for they were coming
in to land. The passengers were already beginning to
stir and collect their belongings and the loudspeaker
made its usual plea for calm.

"Do not leave your seats until the aircraft has come
to a complete stop. Please keep your seat belts
fastened."

The stewardess handed the ticket back. "You got on
the wrong plane at Nice," she said helpfully.

"But what do I do now?" cried Marion.

"Have you a passport with you?"

"No, I haven't. You don't need one to go from Nice to
Paris."

"Then I'm afraid you can't leave the airport."

"But I don't want to leave the airport. All I want is to
reach Paris as soon as I can."

"Yes, Madame, of course. There's a flight at two
o'clock; why not get that? Three and a half hours to
Paris and you're home. All you have to do is buy a
return ticket."

"But I—" Appalled, Marion realized that she had no
money with her.

"You can't? I suppose you could pay by check,
though?" The woman was growing impatient, for the
aircraft had stopped and people were leaving their
seats. "You'll have to make a statement to the airport
police first, but that takes ages, so I don't think you'd
catch the two o'clock flight. Still, you could come back
with us at nine this evening."

The prospect of missing the earlier plane was the last straw.

"Wait, let's see if there's enough in here."

Marion seized the flight bag once more and began frantically going through the wallet.

"I'll say there is!" The stewardess was visibly comforted by the sight of so much wealth. "You only need about 600 francs." She wouldn't have to waste her time straightening this mess out after all and could get on with more amusing things in Málaga.

"You're richer than you thought you were," she beamed. "That makes it a whole lot easier. Wait here, please. When the passengers have all disembarked I'll take you to the office and you can explain what happened and pay for the ticket. They'll probably knock off the Nice-Paris bit. They ought to, anyway; you've paid for it already."

"And there is a plane in two hours?"

"Oh yes, you'll catch it easily. There's bound to be a seat on it; they always keep one or two for these emergencies."

But Marion could not relax until the stewardess had steered her through the necessary formalities and she was finally seated in the plane for Paris.

It might have been worse, she reflected. She had had a certain amount of luck and Florence Montagne would surely forgive her, in the circumstances, for having dipped into her wallet. She would pay her back when she collected her own bag.

If it hadn't been for this idiotic muddle she would have been at Orly airport more than three hours ago. But Stanni wasn't due to arrive from Brussels until late afternoon and since he wasn't meeting her he wouldn't be worried. He would call in at the office on the way home, so he would know nothing about it until she told him. It would make him laugh. Or would he laugh? He might assume his withdrawn look instead: the look he wore when he thought she had done something stupid and didn't want to say so.

Yet, how much more embarrassing it might have been had the flight bag not produced enough to save the day. At least she had not had to go into details with a lot of officials who couldn't understand and probably wouldn't have believed a word she said.

Still, why was Florence carrying all that money? She had counted 2500 francs in the wallet, enough to buy a color TV! It wasn't exactly wise for a young woman to travel with that much cash when checks were so much safer. But she must have her reasons, unless she was one of those rich scatterbrains with no concept of money at all.

Whatever the explanation, Marion was suitably grateful for the windfall. Florence, too, must have had a shock. She would be unable to claim any luggage she might have checked since she wouldn't have the baggage check. Marion hoped she would be waiting under the clock at the Paris airport. Or would she have left a message at the desk? Well, they could get in touch easily enough, since each had the other's name and address. But all the way to Paris Marion worried, trying to fight down the feeling that something was wrong somewhere. It seemed a terribly long journey. They landed at last, however, and she was nearly home. All would be well.

CHAPTER 2

Five-thirty. Her first thought was to retrieve her car,
which must have arrived from Nice by now and to
inquire for news of Florence Montagne. But as she
began her tale the woman at the information desk
pounced on her ticket.

"What's that flight number?" she demanded.

"Four fifty-eight."

"Four fifty-eight?" The echo came in an odd tone
and a startled gaze was fixed on Marion. "Are you
sure?"

"Of course I'm sure. See for yourself." Why, oh why,
was she wasting time like this?

But the other scrutinized the ticket as though it were
something quite incredible, then looked up again,
doubtful and agitated.

"Yes," she said, "so it is."

At once, Marion was uneasy. "What's the matter?"
she asked. Had the owner of the flight bag made a com-
plaint, or concocted some story about the substitution?
The woman's attitude was most peculiar. Now she had

called a companion and both examined the ticket in astonishment.

"You don't know what's happened?"

"No," replied Marion, increasingly alarmed. "What are you talking about? What has happened?"

The two exchanged glances.

"Haven't you seen the papers?"

"Look. I've been to Málaga by mistake. I took the wrong plane from Nice this morning. Instead of coming to Paris, I went to Málaga. And I may tell you that it's cost me—"

The girl cut her short.

"It's saved your life, Madame."

"What?" She looked from one to the other.

"We're trying to tell you how lucky you are. That plane you should have been on—exploded in the air somewhere near Lyons. Simply disintegrated. No survivors."

"No!" she cried, staring at them in dismay.

"Do be careful!" the first woman admonished, "You can't come straight out with news like that. She might have had someone on board, for all you know." She came out from behind the desk and put her arm around Marion, expecting her to collapse at any moment.

"It was just your luggage in the aircraft? I mean, nobody you knew, or anything?"

Nobody she knew. But the lively face, the golden hair under the wide green hat? Tanned and slim and beautiful—how could there be nothing left of Florence Montagne? "Disintegrated." What an awful word; what a sickening, unthinkable picture.

"Nobody you knew, or anything?"

"No, no," she said faintly. "Just my bag".

"Well that's gone, I'm afraid."

Marion began to tremble, hands, shoulders and arms shaking convulsively.

"I think we should take her to the bar," murmured

one of the women. "She needs a brandy or something after a shock like that. Then we'd better notify—"

Abruptly, the shaking stopped. "My husband's the one to notify. He'll be thinking I'm dead, if he's read about it."

Kind as they were, she tore herself from them and made for the exit. "The telephone's the other way," they called, but she did not hear. She had to find a taxi as soon as possible; she had to reach Stanni and show him she was alive. He must have returned back from Brussels at three or four o'clock. If he had not learned of the crash by then, he would certainly have heard the news at the office. What a state he must be in! Damn the phone system and its everlasting delays. They had been in that house now for eighteen months and were still without a telephone, although Stanni had raised heaven and earth to have one installed.

Once in the taxi, she looked at her watch. It was six in the evening, when the traffic was at its worst; it might take an hour or more to reach la Celle Saint-Cloud. She couldn't get through to him at the office, even if he were still there: the switchboard wasn't open after five.

As the shock caught up with her she sat, rigid, in a corner. If it weren't for the confusion at Nice she, too, would be—disintegrated—like Florence. Dust, blowing about in space. Her heart pounding wildly she started to tremble again and shrank in terror. To make things worse, the driver was garrulous and the disaster obviously the topic of the day.

"You wouldn't get me in one of those contraptions," he declared, "not for all the money in the world. Dreadful things. As if there weren't enough ways to kill yourself on the ground, without gallivanting about in the air. It isn't natural. If you're in a car crash, there's some chance of survival; but up there, no way. A hundred and twenty, that's how many went this morning, all at once. Interesting, though, isn't it?"

No, hardly interesting. That was not the word she would have chosen. No more than this wretched man's chatter was interesting, when he ought to be trying to make better time.

"Can't you go any faster?"

"I'm doing my best, lady, you know what rush hour's like. Same all the time, though. It's getting beyond a joke, Paris is. I can't wait for the day when I retire."

Relentlessly he continued, while Marion buried her face in her hands, more and more distraught. Stanni would think she was a ghost. It would be a shock to see her, the sort of shock that could be serious. But he had solid nerves, thank God, and how relieved and thankful he would be afterwards!

And really, what an incredible thing to happen, a miracle, almost. Fantasizing, she began to see herself as the heroine of a fabulous adventure; she rehearsed what she would say to people. Reporters, for instance; they would be thronging round, without a doubt, eager for details.

She looked out at the streets, at lights appearing in shop windows and passersby walking along: a woman with a child lagging behind, a huge sticky sucker in its mouth; a girl with a briefcase—a student, probably; two lovers clinging in a doorway as if they could never part; crowds pouring out of subway stations. Seeing it all, intense joy streamed out through her and she felt herself relax.

That's what life is, she thought, *it's people*. And she was still alive; she still belonged to it. Alive! She was alive! She pressed her palms together, touched the skin of her arms and cheeks in a kind of ecstasy. She was *there*, really, truly there! That was the simple fact, the simple marvel, the miracle. She, who might have been disintegrated, was here instead, still in the world, still with her youth, and her love and her husband. Her husband who would welcome her into his arms, back from the dead in a gray jersey suit. He was grieving at this moment, but soon she would lay her head on his broad shoulder, put her arms around his neck and kiss him as she had never done before.

There would be an end of reserve on his side and of hesitation on hers. He might not be demonstrative, but that apparent coldness was not going to frighten her again—not when she had so nearly lost both him and her own life at the same time. Heavens, how this taxi crawled! How could it dawdle so when she was bringing joy home to a house of mourning? *Faster, please go faster!*

"What number, Madame?" They were there.

"Number seventeen, the gate on the right. Yes, you can stop here." In a near frenzy she paid the man, her eyes devouring the familiar house, the roses on the wall, the bed of giant dahlias, all of it dearer than it ever had been before. To think she might never have seen it again! She could have hugged it all.

A light shone in the first-floor studio. She opened her bag to find her key, then remembered her own wasn't there. Marion, Marion, you must be miles away—what are you thinking of? The keys she wanted were disintegrated, along with everything else. She felt like falling to her knees on the doorstep in sheer thankfulness.

Just in time, she stopped herself ringing the bell. If Stanni came down and heard her voice, saw her standing there in the dusk, goodness knew what he might think. No, she must spare him, break it more gently. Call softly first, then quickly tell him: "Stanni, it's only me. I wasn't in the plane crash. I'll explain in a minute, but here I am. Darling, it's really me."

She walked around to a shed at the back of the house where a spare key was kept for the daily cleaning woman. She found it, entered the house and went up the service stairs to the floor above.

She heard voices. Which of their friends, she wondered, had come to be with him as soon as they learned the news? Her arrival would be like a bombshell—a bombshell of happiness.

The voices were clearer as she stole up the stairs, but she could not yet tell whose they were, nor distinguish what was said. Quietly she opened the door of the studio gallery. The studio occupied two levels; steps from a gallery housing the bookshelves divided the sitting room. It was in the gallery that she now stood, behind the half-open door, invisible to the lower part of the room.

She never knew what kept her there, prevented her from moving forward. But there was an atmosphere, a significant something in the air. And the silence. . . . Suddenly she was aware of silence where there had been a confused murmur of speech.

Then she heard Stanni's firm step and he moved into the light by the table, a pipe gripped in his hand. How well she knew that pipe, and the delicious smell of his tobacco smoke. Home! The customary things of home; how good they were. And yet, he didn't look in the least distressed or upset. Why not? Unless he hadn't seen the paper, didn't know about the crash? Or perhaps he hadn't realized which plane it was?

A second figure came into her view: a woman, leaning forward as Stanni lit her cigarette. The face was vaguely familiar, but who was she? The woman raised her head from the lighter and Marion was able to see her better. Desperately she searched her memory until the answer came: it was her father's secretary. Tall and dark, with brilliant eyes, but always neat and subdued, as though to balance the striking appearance; she had been Félicien Maraval's private secretary for the last

few years of his life, and a very good one, so he used to
say.

What was she doing here? Who could have sent her?
Since her father's death, Marion had never heard her
mentioned; she didn't even know the woman still
worked for the company.

Still she listened to the threatening silence, heavy, it
seemed, with inexplicable sounds; to slow footfalls as
the two actors passed back and forth in the strange
scene that baffled and somehow alarmed her.

The woman spoke and Marion recognized the voice.
In her father's office it had been obliging, deferential;
now it rang with self-assurance and authority.

"I must say, it's beyond me, the way things seem to
turn out for you. All stumbling blocks removed. Fate's
obviously on your side."

"Well, yes. You could say I was lucky."

The words might have been small lethal missiles,
speeding upward. What did he mean, lucky? And they
were talking so intimately together. A wave of apprehension swept over her. Her hands felt suddenly sticky
and she wiped them, unthinking, on her skirt.

"At least we can meet openly now. I was getting
very tired of the hole-and-corner nonsense."

Then Stanni, sounding so natural, as though nothing
out of the ordinary had been said: "What else could I
do? Announce one fine morning, 'By the way, this is
your sister-in-law. Her name's Carole. I know I never
mentioned her, but. . . . ' A bit peculiar, surely?"

"I suppose so, yes. No good, in any case; she's seen me
in her father's office." The woman gave an unpleasant
laugh. "And the old boy would have smelled a rat, too,
if he'd known. There I was, telling him he simply had
to employ this marvelous foreigner, pushing you for all
I was worth, unobtrusively, of course. And there he
was, lapping it up. I used every ounce of influence I had
with him, and believe me, I had plenty. He trusted my

judgment. I fixed the whole thing, from the word go, and he had no idea."

"You were certainly there when I needed you. It was a real port in a storm, that marriage. God knows where I should be if we hadn't pulled it off."

"You'd be in jail," said Carole.

"Oh, hell, don't exaggerate." Stanni sounded angry.

"But, my dear, you would. You know as well as I do you could have been arrested any minute. You were pressed for money; you hadn't a hope of paying people; you were in an awful mess. When I think of how stupid you were, tangling with that phoney promoter, signing checks you couldn't meet, going through cash that didn't belong to you. It was impossible."

"Do we have to go through that again?" His voice grated.

"You took me in too, remember. I gave you guarantees—you had every penny I'd saved. I was liable as well, don't forget. And if there had been any trouble I would have lost my job. The boss was a stickler for principles." She paused and added less stormily, "Still, it worked out in the end. It wasn't easy, but I managed it."

"You were a very clever girl." They were like two crooks congratulating one another. "Introducing me and getting me in there—no problem at all. Genius."

Above in the gallery, with the world rocking around her, Marion shivered. Was this part of the nightmare too? Did disintegration, then, go on forever? The man who said such terrible things in that cold, corrosive tone could not be Stanni. Not the husband she loved and admired, the man other women turned to look at on the rare occasions when he took her out. The man down there was different; something, some inconceivable, fearful power, had changed him.

But the speakers continued the relentless dialogue, unaware of her presence, slowly tearing her to shreds.

"It's true, we were lucky all the way. First, the old boy taking to me like that and handing over his whole advertising operation: well, it helped, for the time being, anyhow. Then his little girl falls for me and we really are in business."

Marion was stunned. How could he? Jeering, insulting—it was unbearable.

"And how you did encourage her!" added Carole, with mocking approval. "I seem to recall a great display of he-man charm."

"No problem there. She was fresh out of school in England, and that must have been hell's own bore. She'd have thrown herself at the first man she met who wasn't positively uncouth. It happened to be me."

Marion felt as though she had been struck. The smell of his favorite tobacco was beginning to make her sick. "Our big break," Carole went on, "was when the old man left us for a better world. Otherwise, my sweet, he'd have sent you packing."

"I don't think so." He sounded so sure of himself. "You're forgetting our cherished Marion. Anything she wanted, she had to have."

"Marion?" Again the insinuating laugh. "You'd have gone no further with her than with Papa, I fear. I'll tell you something now. The very day he had his heart attack, Papa received a report that cancelled you and me out. That's what sped him on his way, I imagine."

"What do you mean? You never mentioned this before!" There was a note of apprehension.

"No. I purposely said nothing at the time. And since your marriage we haven't exactly met seven days a week."

"How could we? But I kept in touch, didn't I? I sent checks."

"And I've earned this pittance you give me. You know very well who put your foot on this particular ladder."

"What a charming couple!" thought Marion, between disgust and despair. Yet her mind took in, with cruel clarity, every word they uttered.

"We've always been in this together," her husband was saying.

"Yes, and that damned report would have finished us completely. Old Maraval was brighter than we gave him credit for. When it came to his darling daughter he wanted to know it was a good, sound young man that she was marrying. He hired a private international inquiry agency to check you out."

"He didn't." Now he was alarmed.

"He did indeed. Never be too sure of yourself; there's always something around the corner. It was a very full report."

"How do you mean, full? What are you driving at?"

"They came up with some fascinating details from your past," she informed him, in the same, mock-dramatic tone.

The pipe knocked nervously against an ashtray. "Dora?" said Stanni, in a flat voice.

"They found Dora."

"Found her? But that means—"

Silence fell. Something terribly important had been said. Marion, trying to make sense of it, was aware of an abyss along whose edge she had been walking with her eyes shut.

"You're sure?" said Stanni . Whatever it was, he didn't want to believe it.

"I told you, I read the thing myself. It's perfectly true."

Another long pause followed, as though each were deliberating separately.

"But I never expected to hear of her again"

"Women can't always vanish to order, just because it happens to suit you, you know."

"I thought she was dead."

A block of ice had formed around Marion's heart. Her head swam.

"You ought to have told me!" came his angry exclamation. "Why didn't you tell me?"

"What was the point? With Maravel dead it wasn't likely to come out, was it? It was all so long ago, and nobody else was interested. I stole the report. Think of the worry it saved you. A decision like that—you might have ruined every plan we had." Carole's voice rose. "We were sitting on a volcano, Stanni; there was only one thing you could do."

"Do for you, you mean. You were thinking about yourself, as usual."

"That isn't true, and you know it. I've always considered your interests, not mine," she replied angrily. "I'm the elder. I've always run the risks, always looked after you. Do you think I'd have bothered, otherwise?"

"Oh, I appreciate all that. I'm not blaming you. I doubt if it would have made much difference if you had told me. I would have gone ahead, just the same."

"Yes, you probably would. Face it, you're a natural-born bird of prey, Stanni. I know you."

"Maybe. I take it as a compliment, in any case." Then, with sudden intensity, "I'm a refugee, remember? And I made up my mind once and for all I wasn't going to be a pauper like the rest of them. I'll have my place in the sun, whatever I have to do to get there."

Quietly as they spoke, the words rose clearly up to the involuntary listener overhead, each word loaded and deadly.

"And now you're there; with the job, and the heiress, and everything you wanted. And you did want her, didn't you?"

"Oh, well; that's something else again."

Why won't my heart keep still, Marion cried to herself in anguish. *What am I going to hear next? What was I thinking of when I married him?*

"But you always thought she was gorgeous!" said Carole in astonishment.

"I thought she was gorgeous when she was the great objective, yes; something to dream about. I wanted her for what she stood for. If she hadn't been her father's daughter I should never even have seen her come into a room. Not my type at all."

"Still, in two years you presumably resigned yourself?"

"I did not. As far as money goes, the marriage was fine. But if you really want to know, the strain was appalling, and it was getting worse."

"But Stanni, why? It can't have been Dora; you forgot her ages ago. Was there anyone else?"

"Everybody else," he said, viciously. "Every woman I set eyes on looked better than the one I had. Who wants to be kept on a short chain and smothered?"

It was as though he was giving vent to the rage inside him, cutting free. "Oh, I thought it might work out to begin with, and married life was not too bad. But having to be the great lover and play up to all the romantic stuff Marion was dishing out with a trowel the whole time—that I couldn't cope with.

"The more she went on billing and cooing, the more she stifled me. The more she was there, the more intolerable it became. It wasn't her fault I couldn't stand the sight of her, of course—but I'm not looking at it from her point of view. I almost hated her, because of why I had married her. That's the way I am—independent. I couldn't bear to wear a collar and a leash."

"God, how awful for you. Didn't she notice anything?"

"You must be joking. She didn't have the brains of a sparrow. She was happy. That kept her busy. Never another thought."

Marion shuddered again. It was true, she had been

happy. But how—on this foundation of deceit and horror?

"I even thought of leaving her, you know."

"Leaving her. You must have been mad!"

"Don't worry, there was too much to lose. Those Maraval perfumes being sold all over the world."

Carole recited the litany. "Lady in Black," "Island Breeze," "Interlude."

"Well, the old man was a marvelous chemist; you have to give him that," Stanni went on," and he left some marvelous formulas. I have a laboratory doing research, quite apart from the firm, and I had them analyzed. I'd decided to float my own company, as soon as I saw my way clear, and sell them in America or somewhere, under my own name."

"And very nice, too, but what about your wife? The formulas were her property. Once she realized you didn't want her, you could have ended up in the courts."

"A wife can't sue her husband for theft, my dear."

There was a soft, admiring whistle. "You thought of everything, didn't you? Congratulations!" said Carole, ironically.

He snapped his fingers in reply. There was no need to think of anything, now.

"Oh, well, I can forget all that," he said. "Marion's gone and I'm the boss—and may she rest in peace! She was nothing to me, really. An episode."

How odd to hear your own epitaph, to feel it branded on your heart. Marion stood, fighting back the tears.

"Rather a hazardous episode, I'd say."

"Perhaps."

They both started. A small noise had come from the gallery.

"Was that a door?" Carole whispered, looking up.

Her brother listened a moment; then shrugged. "No.

Only a draft somewhere. There must be a window open.''

Managing somehow to control herself and keeping carefully out of sight, Marion crept away. She had come as a ghost from the world of ghosts, but it was the real world to which she was going now. She, thank God, was a survivor and the purpose of her survival was to bring these two to book.

The apathy left her and a fever of emotion took its place. Anger, shame and humiliation mingled with her shock and indignation. How had she lived for nearly two years with such a contemptible creature? And without the faintest suspicion, never an inkling of what he was? What had she been *thinking* of?

But now a pitiless light was shed on everything: on her husband's motives and his cunning; on the coldness she had mistaken for reserve; on the liberty he had given her, thankful his own was equally assured; on his refusal to have children.

She had strayed blindly into an alien world and lived there with an unscrupulous man to whom she had been the key to a bank account. A man to whom her death was a godsend. Lucky Stanni. Yes, he had been lucky. But not anymore, she swore to herself; not anymore.

She was shattered and exhausted and had to find a bed for the night. In this one terrible day she had come up against things that would hurt forever. The picture of her dying father would never leave her, his life most probably shortened by the shock of discovering what kind of man his daughter wished to marry.

What, in fact, did he discover? Who was this Dora whose mere name threw brother and sister into retrospective panic? But it had not been chance that prevented her from boarding a doomed airplane. It had been special providence, and she took courage at the thought.

A cruising taxi driver slowed and stopped beside her. He had spotted the flight bag clutched in her hands.

"Taxi?" Then, seeing her haggard face, "Are you all right, Madame?"

She pulled herself together with an effort and said, "I'm tired, I've been walking. What a good thing you came along."

"It's far too late for young ladies to be out walking."

He sounded kind. She climbed in and settled back.

"Where to?" he inquired.

Still shocked, she could only wonder, Yes, *where to?*

The man turned and regarded her uneasily.

"Oh, the Hilton," she said. It was the first hotel she thought of.

IN A ROOM at the Hilton she gave way to despair. She had no home. In her house was a despicable crook who had been her love and her husband. But the very thought of Stanni made her ill again and she rushed to the washroom.

Distress of mind and body together left her whimpering like a hurt child. Pain came back as a toothache reasserts itself when an injection wears off. But for her pain there was no injection, nothing she could take, nothing she could do but sob into the pillow.

CHAPTER 3

The contents of Florence Montagne's bag had produced all she needed for the night, including a mild sedative, thanks to which she managed to get some sleep. For a moment, on waking, she couldn't remember where she was; then the realization and the pain came back together. The scene was etched in her brain; the pitiless, incredible words went around in her head. But gradually, resolve took over. A chance in a million had shown her what Stanni was involved in and she was going to see that he didn't get away with it. She intended to fight.

Innocently, she had been swept into this plot and she had to escape. There was so much she did not understand, but she must know the truth, however unsavory. That might take a long time and a great deal of patience; her husband and his accomplice were not only evil, they were dangerous, and she would need caution. Constantly, the name Dora kept repeating itself, like some sort of alarm bell.

Unfortunately she knew no one she could trust. Her

father had neglected his provincial relations and they did not come to her wedding. When her mother was alive there had been annual holidays with her grandmother in the big white house near Taormina but she hadn't been to Sicily for years. And soon after her mother's death her grandmother, too, had died. The house was sold and the last link with the Sicilian family broken.

No relations to count on. What about friends? But Marion had been educated abroad, so she knew nobody very well at home; and these days her acquaintances were Stanni's friends, not hers. She must beware of them. No, friends were scarce.

However, despite her depressing situation she still held one trump card; no one knew she had survived the plane crash. Her husband and his unspeakable sister thought she was safely dead, never to trouble them again. Their confidence made them drop their guard a little. This, surely, would prove useful in her proposed campaign for freedom and security. She sat and thought and tried to make some plans.

All at once, she was violently hungry: it was twenty-four hours since her last meal. She rang for breakfast and the morning paper, but though she skimmed the pages eagerly, the disaster was not mentioned. Ruefully, she realized that news went stale overnight.

Other and more practical problems faced her. For the moment, all she possessed was the flight bag picked up in error at Nice and rifled shamelessly since; she must draw some money to live on while she waged her battle. On the other hand, she did not want her escape, nor her presence here in Paris, known. Not yet, at any rate; there would be time to announce her existence later. This would have to be solved somehow, but meanwhile the first priority was Florence Montagne's bag. The owner, alas, would never claim it, but there must be a family somewhere. She would try to trace them.

So far, she had been in no fit state to go through the contents methodically, but now she emptied them out onto the bed. Among other things, there was the envelope that had revealed the dead woman's name; it was from a hotel in Cannes where she must have stayed the night before the journey.

The typewritten letter it contained came from a firm called Lassalle, on rue Pergolèse in Paris.

Dear Mademoiselle Montagne,
Everything being now in order and our plans for this operation definitely settled, we enclose a draft, payable on our bank in Nice, for the fee as specified in your contract. You will, however, be starting from Paris and we shall give you last-minute instructions here. May we stress how important it is that you leave without delay?

The letter was signed "G. Lassalle."

Marion considered for a second, made a note of the address and put the letter back. Clearly, her best move was to go to this office, where Florence Montagne must have been well known. There she could explain the switch and someone would take charge of the bag. As for the money she had borrowed, she would undertake to repay it as soon as she knew what her own position was.

Rue Pergolèse contained two parallel rows of boxlike office buildings that seemed to stretch endlessly off to the horizon. Gazing up at the sheer faces of metal and glass, Marion felt rather intimidated by the impersonal austerity of the street. She had moved from the protection of her father to the protection of her husband, both of whom had always insisted on acting as buffers between Marion and the hard realities of business; and now that Marion was alone, truly alone for the first

time, she found the confrontation with reality quite
unnerving.

Biting her lower lip, she took a deep breath and
pushed open the large glass door of the structure that
housed the Lassalle company. The lobby area was alive
with the rushing sound of flowing water and studded
with potted plants that looked exotic and definitely out
of place. Behind the reception desk a friendly-looking
man wearing glasses leaned forward expectantly at
her approach, hastily folding the tabloid he had been
reading and stuffing it under the desk.

Returning his tentative smile, Marion asked, "Where
would I find Lassalle?"

The man swivelled his chair dramatically, extending
an outstretched hand toward the glass partition behind
him that bore the legend "Lassalle Investigations."

"As you can see, Madame," he told her gently, "you
are already here. Do you have an appointment?"

"No, I . . . " she faltered " . . . I have come to return
something. Florence Montagne's flight bag."

At these words, the receptionist's glance leaped, startled, to her face. Reading the shock in his expression,
Marion began to wish she were elsewhere. But, the die
had been cast, and the bespectacled man had rushed,
stammering, into the glass-walled office to announce
her presence. She felt obligated to wait.

Moments later, the receptionist emerged again, a
short, dark-haired woman marching crisply at his
heels. The woman surveyed Marion quickly, her gaze
resting for a second on the blue flight bag; then she
murmured something to the receptionist, turned to
Marion and said briskly, "Follow me, please."

Marion hoped that Lassalle, whoever and whatever
that person was, was less authoritarian than this
young woman who issued such peremptory orders and
moved with such military precision. Marion found her

demeanor even more unnerving than the glass-and-metal canyon outside.

Beyond the glass partition there was not a maze of offices, as Marion had expected, but rather a single large room containing a massive oak desk. As the dark-haired woman offered her a seat, Marion noticed two other doors in the room that presumably led to adjoining offices; she observed the stark whiteness of the walls, broken only by two official-looking diplomas framed behind the desk. To her surprise, the woman sat down behind the desk. Her white suit, but for the pale shadows cast by the lighting overhead, would easily have blended in with the wall, leaving only a head and that mop of raven hair visible beneath the diplomas. Seemingly with great effort, the young woman softened her expression, carefully composing her face into a pattern of sympathy before asking, "Could I see the flight bag, please?"

Without a word, Marion placed it in the centre of the woman's desk. In very businesslike fashion, the woman went through the contents of the bag, extracting in seconds everything of importance it contained—Florence's identification, the letter from Lassalle and the wallet, now approximately 750 francs lighter than it had been when Marion had first picked it up.

The woman rifled quickly through the bills, then cast an inquiring look at Marion that caused her to blurt out defensively, "I had to borrow some of it, but I'll pay it back as soon as . . . as soon as I'm all straightened out." After this lame finish, Marion sank silently back into the cloth-upholstered armchair, biting her lower lip furiously and feeling the heat rush into her cheeks and forehead. She shouldn't have come here in person. She should have mailed the stupid bag to Lassalle.

At last, the woman, apparently satisfied that everything else was there, began stuffing the items back into

the bag. When she had finished, she removed the bag
from the desk, leaning it against the wall behind her
chair, and turned back to Marion.

"Would you mind answering some questions?" she
asked, in a voice that did not seem at all as cold as her
face. Marion mumbled her assent. "First, what is your
name?"

"Marion Mar . . . Maresco." With a start, Marion
realized she had been about to say "Maraval." Her
married name, when she finally pronounced it,
sounded alien to her, like a name she was assuming for
false purposes, and it came out very hard, making the
dark-haired woman look up at her a little strangely.

Driven by curiosity, Marion demanded, "And what
is yours?"

"I thought you knew. You asked for me with such
conviction at the desk. I'm Georgette Lassalle."

"The G. Lassalle of the letter?"

"Of course." The woman had opened a desk drawer
and was now running her finger down a list of names.
"Here it is," she declared, her finger poised halfway
down the page. "I thought I'd seen or heard that name
before."

Mlle Lassalle looked up, a question deep in her dark
eyes. "You were supposedly on that flight. If you will
pardon the wording of this question, Madame, how is it
that you are here in my office, alive, and with Florence's flight bag?" Expecting a long answer, the investigator leaned back in her seat and gazed candidly at
Marion's face.

Marion, meanwhile, was trying to sort out her own
reactions to "the wording of this question." Her inter-
rogator had certainly not offended her by questioning
the fact of her existence, for Marion had been posing
just the same riddle to herself for nearly twenty-four
hours. And the tone of Mlle Lassalle's voice contained
something lacking at the beginning of their interview—

compassion. There was not the slightest trace of accusation in the question, and Marion was a little surprised at that.

For the first time since they had met, Marion met Lassalle's gaze. The eyes at the other side of the desk were dark brown and lively, containing much candor and curiosity, but tempered by a warmth that seemed to radiate from inside the perfectly oval face. It was the warmth that gave Marion the courage to respond to the detective's loaded question.

She told her about the accidental switch of flight bags, about the missed plane and the unscheduled trip to Málaga, and about the reactions of the two stewardesses at Orly airport. Lassalle consulted the list in the desk drawer again.

"But you live right here in Paris," she pointed out relentlessly. "I'm surprised that the newspaper people haven't leaped on your story and covered the newstands of Europe with it. That you survived is a miracle!"

Marion nodded feebly and muttered, "I ... didn't want anyone to know."

At once, Lassalle looked stern again. She shut the desk drawer with exaggerated gentleness and sighed, "There is a reason for this secrecy?"

"I'm afraid so." A pause, then, "How did you know that I live in Paris?"

"The company lists the cities of residence of all the passengers lost," Lassalle responded, shrugging in the direction of the desk drawer.

"You have a copy of the passenger list?" Marion echoed in wonderment.

Lassalle smiled grimly. "When we heard about the accident, I asked for one from the airline, to discover whether Florence was aboard. As an investigator, I do have access to certain types of information."

Suddenly, the legend painted on the glass partition

reappeared in Marion's mind's eye: Lassalle Investigations. She had been too nervous and preoccupied to notice it before; but in the face of this information, some of her confusion melted away.

Marion began making associations she hadn't been able to form before. Lassalle Investigations had an extensive reputation in Paris, and not only because it was run by a woman, although that circumstance made it special, certainly. Lassalle herself had passed her bar examinations before going into her present line of work, and the story had received a great deal of publicity at the time. But the basis for the fame of Lassalle Investigations had been laid in its first year of operation, when a string of armed robberies had been brilliantly solved by the young woman before her in the demure white suit. Lassalle had infiltrated the gang, using disguises and make up, and had veered dangerously close to breaking the law herself in the course of her investigations. It was this courage and daring that had earned her the nickname "The Lady Detective," and with it, the respect of every other investigative agency in the business, as well as the friendship of some highly placed people in the *Deuxième Bureau*, the French national undercover police.

Chance had brought Marion to this office, to the chair in front of possibly the only person in Paris who could help her out of her predicament, and she resolved not to waste her luck.

"Perhaps, perhaps you can help me," she began hesitantly.

Lassalle quirked one eyebrow, leaned forward over her desk again and said confidentially, "Perhaps I can, Madame Maresco."

Marion jumped at the sound of her married name, causing the detective to quirk her other eyebrow.

"Before anything," Marion insisted, "you must promise to keep my survival a secret!"

"Naturally, Madame. If you are hiring me, then everything you tell me is confidential. Secrecy is a very important part of my business."

Marion nodded, suddenly having difficulty breathing normally.

"It's hard to know where to begin," she admitted, after several moments of silence.

"Why not start by telling me why you spent the night in a hotel last night, instead of at your home?"

"How do you know that I did?" Marion asked. Lassalle smiled, then reached into the blue flight bag. In her hand, when she took it out of the zippered compartment, was a book of matches with "Hilton" on the cover in red-and-white script.

"That could be Florence's," Marion pointed out.

Lassalle just shook her head.

"Florence never stayed at Hilton Hotels," she explained softly, "and Florence didn't smoke." Opening the folder, Lassalle showed Marion where two matches had been torn out. "You did spend the night at a hotel."

It was a statement, not a query.

"I had nowhere else to go," Marion stated simply.

"Your husband?" Marion could feel those dark brown eyes studying every twitch of every muscle in her face.

"He was very happy to learn of the . . . accident," she murmured miserably.

"And you wish to keep him happy?"

"No!" Marion's reaction shocked them both by its violence and suddenness. "I mean he mustn't know that I am alive until I'm. . . . " Marion's voice faded out uncertainly.

Georgette Lassalle's keen powers of observation had taken in the multitude of conflicting emotions displayed one by one on her client's face, and she had come to the conclusion that it was too soon to be asking for details. The accident was less than twenty-four

hours old; and in that time, Marion had had the shock
of learning about the accident and her husband's reaction to it. Some people reacted emotionally very
quickly after a traumatic experience, but Marion was
evidently not one of them.

"Meanwhile," said the detective firmly, "you can't
go home, and you lost everything you had with you in
the accident. Now that you've returned Florence's bag,
you have only the clothing on your back. And I suppose
you can't get at your bank account without alerting
your husband. Is that a fair assessment of the
situation?"

"Yes," Marion whispered, cowed by this sudden
sweeping evaluation.

"All right, then." As Marion watched, fascinated,
Georgette Lassalle delved into the blue bag once more
and extracted the lizard-skin wallet. She counted out
200 francs onto the desk, replaced the remaining notes
in the wallet and shoved the stack of bills toward
Marion.

"A loan," Lassalle reassured her. "It and the other
money you borrowed will be included in my bill when
the case is concluded."

Smiling gratefully, Marion gathered up the money.

"Did you register under your own name at the Hilton last night?" Lassalle asked abruptly.

"I think so . . . I don't remember too clearly," Marion
apologized.

"No matter—you're not going back there. Your presence in any hotel in this city would be far too easy to
trace." Once again, Marion felt herself being sized up
by Lassalle; she fidgeted a little under the scrutiny.

"Where can I stay, then?" she asked.

"At my apartment," said Lassalle flatly. "And you're
just about Florence's dress size. Come along. We'll have
you outfitted in a flash."

Obediently, Marion trailed the woman out the door

and into the elevator. In the basement garage, they climbed into a spotlessly white Citroen. And almost before Marion knew what was happening, they were speeding along through a maze of unfamiliar streets where shiny office buildings alternated with tumbledown wooden structures.

Suddenly, they seemed to be out in open countryside; but as they passed the Hippodrome, a race track, Marion knew where they were. They were crossing the southernmost tip of the Bois de Boulogne, at the west end of Paris, and headed toward a cluster of tall, narrow buildings. Georgette Lassalle's apartment was in one of the cluster, although Marion could not figure out which of the four.

The apartment itself was as spotless and white as the car and the office had been, the starkness here being broken by the numerous potted plants that lined the windowsills in the kitchen and living room, and by the splashes of color brought to a mainly black-and-white decor by throw cushions, the two or three small wall-hangings and the huge oriental vase sitting in the middle of the coffee table.

Like the detective herself, the place was neat, methodical, relentless in its insistence on the two extremes of color, and yet softened here and there, holding surprises for the person who took the trouble to walk around and discover them. Marion decided that the hardness and businesslike attitude was a facade, one that had been carefully constructed to ensure her success in a very tough business.

"You'll have to sleep on the sofa," Mlle Lassalle informed her. "However, I've been told it's very comfortable."

Now it was Marion's turn to quirk an eyebrow.

"I must get back to the office," said Lassalle. "I'm meeting a client, but it shouldn't take long. When I return I'll bring some of Florence's clothes for you to try on." And, without waiting for Marion's reaction, Lassalle dashed out the door, leaving her alone for the afternoon.

Suddenly, a terrible weariness seemed to overcome Marion, and she sank down into a black-and-white striped armchair in the living room. On the opposite wall, the only break in its stark whiteness was a pen-and-ink sketch of two young people sitting on a bench, with the huge round fountain of the Tuileries gardens behind them. Gazing raptly into each other's face, they seemed to epitomize romantic love. Marion concentrated on the expression on the girl's face; the longer she stared at it, the sillier it looked, until she felt actual embarrassment on the young woman's behalf that such a ridiculous expression should have been frozen on her face by the artist!

I wonder, Marion thought, *whether I looked at Stanni like that.*

Suddenly, Marion was back at the Christmas party, the one her father had thrown to celebrate the launching of his latest perfume, "Christmas Rose," which he dedicated to his only daughter. How long ago that seemed, but it hadn't been more than three years. Félicien Maraval, an acknowledged chemical genius when it came to mixing fragrances, had brought her home from boarding school in England to start off the publicity campaign, dreamed up by the new advertising manager, Stanislas Maresco.

She had been not quite nineteen, and Stanislas had been twenty-seven, not, strictly speaking, handsome— thin as a greyhound, with an interesting, furrowed look—but undeniably attractive. His pleasing expression and great ease of manner gave the impression of breeding. There was the slightest hint of a foreign accent, and when he smiled, he revealed remarkably strong white teeth.

He had fled, as a student, from some turbulent European country, in what he claimed were tragic circumstances. The sad, mysterious shadow that crossed his face from time to time made Marion's schoolgirl heart turn over; she was fascinated by his "Slavonic charm." The expression, one she had used too frequently before they were married, drew a bitter chuckle as she remembered it.

Amazing, that a person could wear a mask constantly for years at a time! Well, she had seen it crumble away, revealing the hateful monster underneath. And, like a crusading knight, she would bring that monster down, now that she had enlisted the "Lady Detective" in her cause.

The couple on the bench hadn't moved. They gazed rapturously into each other's eyes, intent on finding something there to love, and oblivious to everything around them, just as Marion had been for two years.

That fateful Christmas vacation he had made her feel like a woman, causing her to scorn the boys her own age she had been content to flirt with until then. And the places he had taken her!

With Stanislas Maresco, she had seen the inside of a gambling den, several lavish dinner clubs and the Folies-Bergère, all during that wild, whirling week! Her mother had died when Marion was thirteen and after attending a boarding school for five years, Marion Maraval soon became more familiar with the English countryside than with the outskirts of her home city, Paris. Visiting all the exciting nightspots and attending cultural events with Stanislas made her feel like a tourist on the deluxe tour. Even the Louvre, that massive, hulking art museum, came alive when Stanislas guided her through it.

Remembering those carefree days Marion sighed. Deluded by her infatuation for Stanni, she had enjoyed herself with him. In some ways, perhaps ignorance *was* bliss.

Félicien Maraval had doted on his daughter, but he had always been too busy with his burgeoning perfume business to pay much attention to her. Perhaps, if he had been more of a disciplinarian. . . .

No, Marion realized now, it wouldn't have made any difference. Stanni had been courting her for one reason only, and he would have found some way to marry her, even if her father had objected strenuously to their first dates.

Or perhaps if their family had been a little closer, if there had been a female relative she could have turned to for advice.

Marion's mother had been born in Sicily, and her only relatives were some cousins and an aunt near Palermo. There were other, distant kin on her father's side, but they lived in the country, and he had barely kept in touch with them. The Maraval family had been an island in Paris living the urban life that all the rest of the family on both sides, found distasteful. With her mother's death, and then her father's, that island had been eroded away to the pitiful rock that was Marion Maraval Maresco.

Marion sighed tremulously and brushed away an incipient tear with the back of her hand. Her father had never seen her growing up—she'd done all that in England. As far as he had been concerned, her wish to marry the advertising manager was nothing more than a girlish whim, one that would fade away as soon as she was safely packed off to school again. Nevertheless, when her headmistress wrote him enquiring whether he approved of the correspondence between his daughter and this "boyfriend," he was worried.

To be sure, he had nothing against Maresco, who was good at his job and could talk prospective clients around in no time. Stanislas was discovered by his own private secretary, Carole Jordan, whose husband had worked for the firm before his death, and on whose warm recommendation Maraval had given him a trial. But there was a big difference between giving someone the advertising account and handing him your daughter.

That was why he had engaged the investigative firm to look into Maresco's background; and what they had uncarthed, according to Carole Jordan, had triggered his fatal heart attack.

Marion smiled crookedly at the memory of Stanni meeting her at the airport after she had learned of her father's death. He had been so very sorry, so sincere, so willing to take care of everything for her. How unbelievably efficient he had been! And how heavily she had leaned upon him in her time of bereavement! But what had done the trick, what had cast her heedlessly, headlong into Stanislas Maresco's trap, were his words to her after her father's funeral: "He told me he was ill, the last time we talked. He asked me, then, if I would look after you. I gave him my promise, and I intend to keep it."

Disregarding all advice to wait, Marion knew only that she was lonely and unhappy, that she missed her father dreadfully and that she was more in love than ever. What was wrong with marrying?

What could she have been thinking of, dreaming about? Finally, overhearing that appalling discussion had broken the dream forever and disclosed a world of lying and deceit such as she had never known existed; it was an ugly, hostile world, where nothing was solid and she could hardly breathe or move.

GEORGETTE LASSALLE CAME THROUGH THE DOOR at three-thirty in the afternoon, to find Marion staring with tear-filled eyes at her sketch of the two lovers in the park. Laying the several dresses and skirts down gently on the sofa, she slipped into the adjacent striped chair. Now was the time to pursue the details of this client's case.

"Marion," she prodded gently, "are you hungry?"

The only answer was a sorrowful shake of the head.

"Marion, look at me," Lassalle commanded her. Slowly, the head turned until the two gazes met; at that instant, Marion burst into tears, a luxury she had been unable to indulge until then. Lassalle patted her on the shoulder and made soothing sounds until the wrenching sobs subsided, ten minutes later, and Marion was able to speak.

"Thank you, I feel much better now."

"Good," the woman said emphatically. "Feel like talking?"

Marion thought for a second and had to concede that, yes, she certainly did feel like unburdening herself to Georgette Lassalle. She was finally able to give a coherent account of all that had happened on that long, eventful day.

But , Marion wanted to know the full story; that terrible couple had to be dealt with somehow.

"There's so much I simply cannot understand. They were talking about my marriage as if I should not have been married at all. And Dora, who's she? I never even heard of her before. It's like being in a quagmire, with everything giving way under you."

Lassalle had listened without interruption. Now, she shook her head. "It's a dreadful mess, I agree, but not hopeless. Given time and patience everything can be solved in the end. The worst thing is, of course, that you are married. Your husband has legal authority over you and your money; for the moment, anyway. He can certainly deny anything you say you overheard. He never told you he had a sister, but that's no crime; he'd manage to justify it, one way or another. And once he discovers you know the truth, he'll certainly come up with something. He strikes me as a very clever and very dangerous man."

"Dangerous, I'm sure of it," added Marion.

"It was a good thing you had the presence of mind to stay out of sight; it took courage to keep quiet through such a nightmare."

"I couldn't have moved. It was as though I'd been drugged or something."

"Well, it's an advantage, in any case, and we mustn't waste it. Surprise is our strong suit right now." Georgette Lassalle took on a calculating gleam in her eyes. She stood slowly and moved to the coffee table, where she reached into the vase and took a pencil and a pad out of it.

"Now, there's the firm. Your father founded it and left it to you; your husband's running it. Have you decided what to do with it?"

"Oh, sell it!" Marion was angry and bitter. "I want to sell it and send him packing. I was mad to let him get his hands on it. They've made God knows what out of it, he and his sister, and I never want to hear of it again."

"In that case, do you know of a lawyer who could deal with that and protect your interests?"

Marion reflected a moment.

"Yes, there's my father's solicitor, Monsieur Perdrière. He's always been very loyal to the family. He warned me not to marry Stanni. Oh, God, I wish I'd had the sense to listen to him!"

"Try not to dwell on the past," said Georgette gently, "while we sort out the present—not a very easy job, I may say. Monsieur Perdrière must be contacted as soon as possible, so he can immediately initiate proceedings and let your husband know what you have decided."

Marion shrank back into her chair. "As soon as Stanni knows that, he'll try to bully me into going back to him. And I won't, I just won't!"

"Don't worry—you won't see him, and he won't see you, especially while we are collecting evidence. Until you have enough to apply for a separation, you can give me power of attorney, and I'll see to it all."

"You mean you'll visit Monsieur Perdrière and—"

"Absolutely everything."

Marion heaved a huge sigh of relief.

"Thank you so much. But then, what do I do meanwhile?"

"You vanish."

"Vanish?"

"That's right—so your husband can't get at you or pester you."

"He's very persistent," Marion pointed out.

"Perhaps, but we are very clever," was the rejoinder. "First, we'll obtain a doctor's certificate stating that you have a nervous condition after your terrible experience and that you must be alone—away from everything and absolutely everybody. Secondly, have you thought about how you are going to pay me for my preliminary work?"

"What a time to bring that up!" Marion blurted out.

The detective raised an index finger to stop her protests.

"It's all part of the plan. You see, I've done some research on you this afternoon. You used to spend time with your mother's family in Sicily, which means you have some Italian. Correct?"

"Correct."

"There is a way that you can go someplace where nobody would even think of looking for you, because you've never been before and you have no friends or family there."

Marion was intrigued.

"Where is this enchanted place?" she asked.

"Sardinia. Florence Montagne was to begin an assignment for me there before she was killed." Lassalle reached into her handbag and withdrew the lizard-skin wallet with the rest of the notes in it. Extending it to Marion, she said, "This is yours, if you'll take Florence's place. It's the fee for the assignment."

Remembering the sort of assignments that Georgette Lassalle usually took on, Marion felt her knees go weak.

"But what makes you think I'm even remotely capable of doing whatever it is?"

"I'm not suggesting anything that is dangerous or beyond your abilities. And it's nothing illegal, even if the methods seem a bit unorthodox. Have you ever heard of Paulette Arnaudy?"

"The singer? Yes, of course I know of her. She has a beautiful voice and a great career."

Lassalle smiled enigmatically. "This assignment is to retrieve something of hers that was stolen. She and I will take care of the retrieval—all you have to do is give us information about the location of the . . . object."

"That's all?"

"All. She and I will take all the risks, you have my word. Meanwhile, for several weeks at least you would be abroad, in a place where nobody would think of looking for you. Well what do you think?"

Marion thought for a moment. If all she had to do was gather information. . . .

"All right," she said, "but I want more information before I commit myself completely."

"Paulette Arnaudy is as engaging a personality off-stage as she is on," began Lassalle with a smile. "You know what she looks like, obviously, since her picture appears on the dust jacket of every record she sells—it's in her contract."

Marion nodded, visualizing that long wavy fall of chestnut hair, that soft complexion, those sultry eyes and pouting mouth that had become synonymous with the name Paulette over the years.

"Anyway," Lassalle continued, "she married a Sardinian five or six years ago, and he gave her a daughter. His family disowned him or something when he married her, because she was an entertainer. But when he died of cancer, about three years ago, they suddenly decided that they wanted his daughter. The French courts awarded her custody of the little girl, but that wasn't good enough for the family. One of the men of her husband's family sneaked into France one day three years ago and stole the child."

Marion, deprived of the joy of children herself, could well imagine the wrenching pain in a mother's heart to realize that her only child had been taken from her.

"Finally, after all this time, there is an opening for us to get the child back," declared Lássalle, "and you are going to fill that opening. The family has decided to hire a governess for the little girl. I had already arranged for Florence to be hired, but since she is unable to take the job, and you speak some Italian, it would be just as easy to have them hire you. Your assignment would be to discover what routine, if any, the family follows; to fill us in on the members of the family; and, of course, to do the job for which they would be hiring you—to look after the child and teach her."

After a momentary pause, Marion said, "I think I could handle that."

Lassalle went on vigorously. "During that time, I would be conducting an investigation on your behalf, and I would, of course, keep you informed of my progress. All you have to do is return the favor."

"Yes," said Marion, beginning to smile herself now.

"Then come try on some of these clothes," suggested Georgette, scooping them up and leading the way into the bedroom.

CHAPTER 4

With a jarring of brakes, the ancient Fiat stopped at a postern gate and the driver announced that they were there.

"You mean this is it?" cried Marion, in tones of disbelief. "This is Castel Terralba?"

"This is it," he said, climbing out to open the passenger door.

"But the house? Where do they live?"

"There, in front of you. Those towers, can't you see?"

"People actually live there? How can they? It's a ruin."

"The Terralbas do, the Marquis and the family. One of our oldest families, they are. Just ring the bell, they won't eat you."

She had never seen anything remotely like this stony setting. It was prehistoric, something out of a dream, with its heaped boulders, stone towers and fortresses, tall keeps of stone and high, sheer rocks. Some mad novelist had created it for a tale of romantic horror, all Punic remains and massive, cyclopean walls. Yet men lived here and worked the land, for beyond it lay olive groves and fields of maize and rows of vines. A huddle of flat-roofed houses provided shelter for them.

By now the taxi had turned and rattled away down the pebbly road. There was nothing left to do but pull the bell chain that hung beside the gate. Marion felt suddenly lonely and terrified. She did not actually want to run away, or abandon the job she had come to do, but it was going to take some courage. She was simply not adventurous enough for this sort of thing; the unknown terrified her. Panic was taking over before she even started.

Nevertheless, she pulled the iron chain again, more resolutely this time. Jangling in the quiet, the bell woke echo upon echo from the sun-baked stones, and pandemonium broke out within. Doors banged, dogs barked, a loud, harsh voice was heard. Then footsteps approached over the flagstones. Finally one half of the huge door opened and a man stood peering out.

"Yes?"

Clad in peculiar, outlandish costume, he gave the final touch of unreality, and she had to summon all her remaining spirit to announce, "I'm the new governess. I think they are expecting me."

Her Italian was by no means perfect, but he seemed to gather what she meant. "The chauffeur was supposed to meet you at the station."

"No one met me."

"Still drunk from the festa, most probably," he sighed. "It was St. Michael's day yesterday. Don't know why they bother to employ Sicilians. Come in. I'm the porter, Giuseppe."

He stood back, picked up the suitcases and preceeded her into the vast courtyard. At closer quarters, the buildings were not the ruins they had appeared from outside. Castel Terralba had obviously been restored with an eye to comfort.

At a shout two maids emerged, wearing the long dark dresses, bright embroidered aprons and bodices, typical of this part of Sardinia; though Giuseppe outshone them easily in leggings of goatskin and an abbreviated kilt over white breeches. To greet the new arrival and carry the luggage he had also donned his *berretto*, a cap with a dangling point that swept to the shoulder.

It can't be true, it's pure musical comedy! thought Marion. Stealing sidelong, friendly glances at her, the two girls led the way into a wide hall from which rose a great stone staircase with a handsome bronze handrail. As the black skirts rustled up the steps ahead she gazed around at the colorful images. Magnificent paintings and rainbow panels of tapestry touched the cold stone with warmth and brilliance.

Still with their delighted smiles, the maids ushered her into a turret room where the same vivid contrast of color and sunshine against gray stone walls greeted her. The hangings, the covers, an elaborate shawl flung across the carved wooden frame of the bed: all were luminous, blazing. Rush-work chairs with cushions and bright rugs on colored tiles completed the effect. The windows were narrow and so high that she had to stand on a footstool to see out. And for good measure a tapestry-lined door led to a tiled bathroom fit for a Moorish queen; two steps led to a sunken bath, inlaid with blue mosaic. She had somehow strayed into a world utterly unlike anything she had ever known.

She returned to the bedroom, looked sadly at her bags and sank into a chair wondering, yet again, "What have I come here for?" But she was about to meet the Terralba ladies; now was no time for second thoughts.

She was here to help another, equally friendless and unhappy woman recover her dearest treasure, the child who had been stolen from her. She had accepted a certain amount of risk, and this was where it started.

But she felt apprehensive and alone and not entirely unafraid, for she knew something about the people she was up against. Here in the lion's den she was invading their territory. She steeled herself to face them and went downstairs.

Entering the enormous drawing room, Marion was too petrified to take in any details, conscious only of the tall, imposing woman who advanced to greet her. At once the woman inquired, in very poor French, whether she spoke Italian.

"A little," Marion replied. "That is, I understand it."

This was apparently good enough and it was in Italian that the Marchesa introduced herself, before saying, "And this is the Dowager Marchesa, my mother-in-law."

From the far end of the room a hoarse, commanding voice uttered the words "Come here!" but as Marion, in some alarm, moved in the direction of the summons she heard the sound of wheels. The old Marchesa advanced toward her in a wheelchair. Gimlet eyes glittered from beneath the folds of a black lace mantilla.

"You should have been here yesterday." It was an accusation.

"I was held up, I'm afraid. The agency sent a message. I hope you received it."

"No," said the first Terralba lady, "but our mail service is not very reliable. Do please sit down." She indicated an armchair.

The hoarse voice said something in an unintelligible dialect.

"My mother-in-law wishes to know how you got here."

"By air to Olbia and then to Núoro by train. I stayed the night there and took a taxi the rest of the way."

The old woman's stare was disconcerting and to avoid it Marion studied the younger woman as she rose to fetch a file from a spiral-legged cabinet. She had a severe, regular profile and must have been a great beauty. One white lock shone in her black hair and the snowy mantilla fell, in Sardinian fashion, like a dazzling cascade to her shoulders and over the bosom of her sober silk dress. The set of her head and the curve of her lips were proud; deep lines ran to either side of her mouth and her large eyes were dark-ringed. Close up her face looked older and more careworn than Marion had first thought.

"I take it that the person we originally engaged could not come?" She accompanied the words with a small, polite smile, as though to excuse the inquiry.

"She couldn't, no," said Marion. The true reason for Florence's absence had not been given and she did not enlarge upon her brief explanation.

"Well, how lucky we are that you could step in right away," said the Marchesa, opening the file on her lap.

Wishing the Dowager Marchesa would turn her piercing eyes away, Marion fidgeted where she sat, profoundly uneasy. Surely she would be unmasked, thrown out, handed over to the police; they would accuse her of all sorts of dark designs. It had been ridiculous to come and she saw in a blinding flash what the consequences might well be. How could she have let herself be persuaded into doing any such thing? *Oh God,* she demanded, not for the first time, *what was I thinking of?*

When the old Marchesa rolled her chair to one of the windows Marion relaxed a little, feeling rather less like a specimen insect pinned for an entomologist to study. At last she looked about her.

Triple windows on two sides of the room before rich, heavy curtains and leather-upholstered window seats. On a massive bureau of carved wood, freshly waxed and shining, stood a huge vase of bougainvillea, the purple red flowers spilling over in trusses of brilliant color. Behind it on the wall hung the portrait of a very young man, slim and lithe as a bullfighter. The Marchesa saw her look at it and something like a shadow passed over the serene, controlled face. "My son," she said, "your pupil's father."

Of course, the child. For the moment Marion had forgotten about the child, the purpose of her own presence in this exotic castle.

"Oh, may I see her?" she asked, eagerly grasping the opportunity to end this awkward tête-à-tête.

"Yes, if you wish."

From behind came more gruff, incomprehensible phrases. The mistress of Terralba replied with almost deferential courtesy, rose and held the door open, and the invalid rolled her chair out of the room. Marion breathed a sigh of relief; now she had only one adversary to deal with, the less formidable of the two.

"I have your records here, and your references." The Marchesa looked up. "They really are excellent, excellent."

Marion was aware of being assessed, estimated. As for her recorded achievements and references, she knew they were excellent, for under Georgette Lassalle's direction she had copies of all the documents forwarded to Castel Terralba from an agency in Switzerland.

"It isn't too difficult to teach small children," she rejoined. "They absorb things easily and they learn so quickly."

Even as she spoke, she began to feel better. And why, indeed, should she let herself be overawed? These people had robbed a woman of her child and behaved like brutal despots merely because they were rich and could do as they chose. This Marchesa and her husband, however honorable and dignified they might appear, were cynics who rode roughshod over other people's rights and planned a kidnapping like any pair of villains.

The fact that the child in question was their own granddaughter was quite irrelevant. Their conduct was barbarous. Terralba was a common bandit, but because he was who he was, no one had called him to account. She could intervene without scruple to help restore the poor baby to her mother.

The poor baby, however, seemed not to realize, as yet, that anything was amiss. She proved to be an enchanting five-year-old, plump and pretty and high-spirited, with a little face, dark hair, skin like a peach and bright, intelligent eyes. She held out her hand and said *"Bonjour"* without being told.

"Her accent isn't very good, I know," said the Marchesa apologetically, "but the maids speak Sardinian to her all the time and she tends to forget her French. We don't want that to happen, so really all I would like you to do is talk to her and teach her to read in French. And go gently, don't press her. She's an orphan, you see, and we wouldn't like her to be worried or upset."

"Truly an orphan?" Marion asked, directly. "I mean, both her mother and father are dead?"

"Both." It was abrupt, dry and positive. The subject was unmistakably closed.

Marion turned to the little girl.

"What's your name?"

"Lucy."

As soon as the word was out a finger flew to her mouth and she looked at her grandmother out of the corner of her eye. That lady assumed a scolding expression and corrected her.

"Not Lucy, darling. Luciana."

"Luciana," came the obedient echo, then a gurgle of laughter, as though this were some huge joke.

"We are very particular about the Italian form of her name," said the Marchesa. "Please make sure you use it." In a softer tone she added, "You must be tired—I'll let you go now. Have the rest of the day to yourself, to settle in. I hope you like your room?''

"It's charming, thank you, and it looks very comfortable.''

"Oh, very simple comfort, I'm afraid. We're right up in the mountains here. All the modern luxury's down on the coast and in the tourist places; it hasn't reached us yet. Still, we do what we can. If there's anything you want, just ask the maids.''

The new governess thanked her again and rose, glad that the conversation was over. Looking back from the doorway, she saw that Luciana had scrambled onto her grandmother's knee and that the Marchesa, sat stroking the dark curls tenderly. Her stern face was transfigured; she was blissful. *She really loves that child,* Marion told herself, and her appointed task seemed suddenly less simple.

But what a deplorable situation. Walking down the long corridor to her room, she went over the events of the last hour. She now knew two of those involved in this drama she was involved in, but there remained another hurdle: she had yet to meet the present, impenitent chief of the clan, the redoubtable Marchese who had actually carried Luciana off. Here, in this castle, he was master; he was going to be the most dangerous, the most frightening of the three. The old Dowager Marchesa was certainly a force to be reckoned with—those eyes had, all too evidently, seen right through her from the very first.

Marion felt, instinctively, that the Marchesa was the weak link. The others were real Terralbas: ruthless, irreconcilable, fierce as the savage peaks among which they lived in their eagles' eyrie, centuries behind the times. Yes, those were the two she had to guard against.

CHAPTER 5

M. Perdrière was a tall, graceful man, whose thinning white hair crowned a high, smooth forehead. Although a man of some bulk, he moved with deliberation, economizing every gesture, and this tendency gave him a much lighter appearance. It also, he had discovered, pleased his clients, for they felt that he would exercise the same restraint in the handling of his court cases and, perhaps, in his billing as well.

Perdrière's office was not large, a fact that surprised many people who were aware of his reputation and importance in the Paris legal community. Nor was it situated among the clusters of skyscrapers that had recently sprung up around the western outskirts of the city, although most of his clients had relocated there.

He made them come and ferret him out of a cubby-hole nestled almost exactly in the center of the city, a stone's throw from the Palais de Justice. Granted, it was a luxuriously appointed cubbyhole—paneled in dark walnut, lined with handcrafted bookshelves and rather strongly dominated by a massive hand-carved

desk of the Louis Quatorze style, with ball-and-claw
feet. The matching chair rolled silently on casters
across the Persian carpet.

There was a warmth, a privacy in that office that
couldn't be found at any price in those transparent
towers on the fringes of the city. M. Perdrière had set
up his law practice here almost forty years ago because
he couldn't afford to move, although certainly not for
monetary reasons.

From the moment the red-headed secretary outside
had told Georgette Lassalle she could enter, her keen
eye had taken all this in, and she stood quietly before
Perdrière's desk, looking around and nodding in satisfaction. The lawyer, an amused grin on his face, interrupted this inspection by asking abruptly, "Do you
approve? Please sit down, Mademoiselle."

Lassalle's gaze flickered to his face and she smiled
back as she moved toward the indicated chair. "Very
much so, Monsieur. It isn't my style, but it
has . . . panache."

The old man nodded his acceptance of the compliment, then, adjusting his horn-rimmed glasses, he
cleared the center of his desk symbolically, folded his
arms on its edge and said, "Since receiving your telephone call earlier, I have been asking myself why Mademoiselle Lassalle would want to see me. Is one of
your clients perhaps suing one of mine?"

Lassalle opened a slim briefcase and removed the
papers Marion had signed that morning. She glanced
through them briefly, making sure that they were all
there, before laying them on the cleared area of Perdrière's desk.

"Not exactly, Monsieur Perdrière. As your inspection
of those documents will suggest, one of your clients is
suing another of your clients."

Gingerly picking up the sheaf of papers, Perdrière

glanced briefly at the uppermost one. With a shocked expression he let them drop once again onto his desk.

"Is this a hoax?" he demanded hoarsely. "Her will is being probated!"

"Then the probating will have to stop," said Lassalle serenely, "for the lady is not dead."

Perdrière's glassy brow began to furrow as he leaned pensively back in his chair.

"Marion has signed over power of attorney to me in order to keep her present location a secret. My function in this case is a purely investigative one; and I am to act in her place in all dealings with you." As the expression on the old man's face cleared, Lassalle continued, "She said you were the only lawyer she could trust to protect her interests."

"I served her father's interests for . . . a long time. When her husband came to me asking that the will be expedited through the courts, only twenty-four hours after Marion's death. . . . "

"Alleged death," Lassalle corrected him. "Every one of those signatures has been properly witnessed and notarized. The documents are genuine. And the requests they make are genuine and well thought out."

Perdrière had begun leafing through the assembled papers, murmuring the occasional "Ah?" as he did so. He noted that they were all dated that same morning. At last, he looked up. Lassalle had not changed position or facial expression.

"If you still doubt their authenticity, I can arrange for Marion to telephone you this afternoon and verify what I have told you."

"That won't be necessary. Everything seems to be here—power of attorney, disposition regarding what she overheard the evening of the accident, formal request for a legal separation from her husband, notification of her intent to sell her father's firm and all patents. . . . "

As he pronounced these last words, Perdrière began to smile. "Yes," he repeated with some emphasis, "everything is here."

Remembering what Marion had told her of Perdrière's fatherly interest in her after the death of her parent, Lassalle could well understand that smile. At last, the daughter of his late friend was escaping the swamp she had been mired in for two years. It was the smile of a happy and relieved father. Then, Lassalle shook herself mentally. She had business to transact, and she'd best get on with it.

"Just one last thing, Monsieur Perdrière," she said in a brisk voice. "I understand that before his death Félicien Maraval engaged a firm of private investigators to look into the background of his prospective son-in-law. Their report has been . . . shall we say, mislaid? Since it could be germane to my client's case, any assistance you could give me in locating this firm would be invaluable."

"Unfortunately," the old man said, shaking his head ruefully, "Félicien did not consult me in this matter. He was a very proud man. If the investigation had turned up nothing bad about Stanislas Maresco, he would have been embarrassed to admit to anyone that he had even ordered it. It is safe to assume, however, that he would have engaged only a large, reputable firm with international connections. Félicien Maraval always believed that important undertakings should be done properly."

Lassalle had already deduced all of this. There was a list of company names and addresses in her briefcase. With a sigh, she stood, signaling the end of their interview, and reached across the huge walnut desk to shake M. Perdrière's hand.

"Thank you, Monsieur," she said simply. "I shall be contacting you from time to time."

And with that, she was gone.

Perdrière sank back into the leather-upholstered chair behind his desk and gazed for a time at the documents on his desk. Somewhere in there, he was convinced, was the noose that would hang Stanislas Maresco. The smile broadened, spreading recklessly across his entire face.

For Mlle Lassalle had misread it—Perdrière was not wearing a relieved, paternal smile, but rather, a gleeful, vindictive smile, in anticipation of the moment when he broke the news to that grasping gigolo of his impending eviction from the life of Marion Maraval.

Chapter 6

Thanks to her now-essential sleeping pills, Marion slept well and was up early next morning. Teaching would be a complete change and she was prepared to enjoy it. Breakfast was delicious—as had been the fruit and pastries of the previous evening, sent to her room on a big flat woven platter. The local flour was superb and the pastry cook an expert. All in all, she was feeling much better by the time one of the maids appeared to show her the way to the nursery.

Luciana greeted her with enthusiasm. She was being dressed by a grave-looking girl wearing the usual colorful costume, who told Marion, as she finished, that prayers had not yet been said.

Castel Terralba was clearly a pious household. Around almost every neck there hung a cross or a holy medal on a chain of gold; here in a niche was a small altar bearing a silver Virgin and on the wall above the bed a figurine of St. Lucy stood in a circular frame of some rare wood. And this, too, was curious: for this devout family had acted like a bunch of marauding pirates; how did they reconcile that with their religion?

The nursery was light and cheerful, full of toys and little figures; the straw or carved animals were beautifully made, with marvelously expressive faces. It was a wonderland of a room. She would love it, thought Marion, if she were the child who lived here.

Luciana was hugging a big wooden dog, to which the craftsman had given an air of animated puppy mischief.

"What do you call him?"

"Pippo."

"He's nice. Hasn't he a funny face? Who gave him to you?"

"Carlo."

"Well, Carlo must be very clever, making a dog like that. Is that what he does, carves animals and things?"

Luciana found this amusing and began to laugh. She seemed a naturally merry child, always on the brink of laughter and visibly well and happy. The mother who missed her would have been surprised, chagrined perhaps, to see how well and happy. But children have a discomfiting way of settling down, like small animals, anywhere their wants and wishes are provided for, and whatever the child's mother thought, Luciana was genuinely beloved and properly looked after by her father's people. In the circumstances, this didn't make Marion's role any easier.

But the fact remained that she had been stolen from her mother, and that was wrong, however happy she was. In any case, Marion told herself, how can a child know what is best for it? For the time being, all she wants is material care but later, as she develops and starts to experience the outside world, she'll need her mother most. The mother's cause was Marion's. Had she not longed for children, too?

She thought of the child she had wanted so much,

the pain that lay beneath all she ever said or did. Stanni's face rose before her and again she heard him and his sister pronounce her epitaph—those few contemptuous words that wiped her out of the land of the living, almost as her father had been wiped out, and just as casually.

Yet surely that precious pair would be worried now. By now her husband knew she had survived the explosion. He must be wondering what had come over her, where she had suddenly found the strength and determination to escape his hitherto unassailable, unchallenged influence. Well, let him worry. She knew Stanni; if he met an obstacle, he liked it dealt with and cleared away at once. To have this particular obstacle simply melt into thin air, to be able to do nothing must be driving him mad.

He couldn't possibly suspect her real motives, but he had a nagging problem, all the same. He had always manipulated events to suit himself; now she had gone off and he was losing control of the situation. Control, indeed, had passed to her. He and his accomplice, after believing that the tedious constraints were over, must be a whole lot less secure, if not secretly terrified; and she could not help feeling rather pleased to think of it.

Earnestly, Luciana set about her prayers at the nursery altar. The Our Father and Hail Mary she recited in Sardinian; then in French she went through a list of special people: "Please God, bless—" and a whole string of names, including those of Pippo and Carlo and ending up with, "and please take care of Daddy in heaven."

"Aren't you forgetting someone?" asked Marion.

"Who?"

"Mummy. Your Mummy."

"My Mummy?" She gazed in astonishment.

"Yes."

"She's in heaven, too?"

"You've forgotten her in your prayers," answered Marion, avoiding the question. "Shall I say it for you?"

"Yes."

"You say it after me, then. Please God, take care of Mummy and make her happy."

She was interrupted by a voice like thunder. "You'll say no such thing!"

Luciana cried out and Marion, kneeling beside her, looked around and sprang to her feet. A man glowered at her from the doorway. As he strode into the room and stood over her, she shrank back as if he were going to hit her.

"Never say that again, do you hear?" He spoke in fury, every syllable distinct and separate. All she could do was gasp, "But what's the matter? I don't understand—"

"There's nothing to understand," he shouted, keeping his blazing eyes upon her and tugging the bell cord until it nearly broke. Luciana burst into tears and immediately he spoke to her, affectionately, in Sardinian. Then Francesca, her nurse, came in and at his order picked her up. With an angry glance at Marion she bore her away, struggling and crying in the mysterious dialect, "Carlo" being the only word distinguishable. The door shut behind them. Marion was alone, it seemed, with a maniac.

She forced herself to inspect him calmly: a tall man, in breeches and riding boots, with a lock of hair that fell across his forehead and made him look fiercer still. He brushed it back as his face cleared, and she saw that his eyes, which had been blank with anger, were actually blue. Then he came to himself with a start, as though suddenly aware of her presence.

"Did I frighten you? I'm not really an ogre," he said.

The color returned to her cheeks. "Well, you look less like one now," she responded, hoping she sounded less nervous than she felt.

"Forgive me, please."

The fire was out, but there was nothing humble in his apology. She decided to take the offensive.

"What ever possessed you to behave like that? And who are you, anyway?"

"And you—who are you? You must be Luciana's governess."

"Then I presume you are Carlo? The one who carves the animals?"

She smiled at the thought of the animals, and though they evoked no answering smile, the words somehow served to lighten the atmosphere.

"Didn't the women tell you?"

"What women? Whom do you mean?"

"The women of our house. Oh, it's a perfectly respectful way to speak of them, I assure you. We honor women in Sardinia and the word retains a proper value. I mean the Dowager Marchesa and the rest of the family."

"I've only been here since yesterday. I had a short interview with the two ladies, that's all, and I began my work this morning."

"Nevertheless, you should have been told," he repeated harshly.

He spoke very good French, with what might have passed for a faint southern intonation—a hint of Provence, perhaps.

"Told about what?" she asked quietly.

"About your duties."

"The Marchesa told me. I am to speak French with Luciana and teach her to read it."

"More to the point is what you are not to do." He spoke with command and emphasis.

"And what am I not to do?" She held her ground before him with her nose in the air, being carefully rude and determined to keep her temper and courage as best she could.

"Under no circumstances are you to mention Luciana's mother."

"Oh, why not?"

"Luciana's mother is dead."

"Then surely—"

"Dead so far as she is concerned. Dead to everyone under this roof."

It was on the tip of Marion's tongue to inquire how any mother could be dead to her small daughter just because a pack of domineering relatives chose to say she was. But she bit back the retort, fearing to arouse suspicion in this aggressive person, whoever he might be. Nor must she seem to take sides in a family affair.

"I didn't know."

"Well, you know now. And thank God," he added, half to himself, "that I came in. We have been doing our best to shield that child from disturbing influences ever since—well for quite a long time. You could have done untold damage."

"I am so sorry," said Marion, sarcastically. "I must try to carry out your instructions in future. Providing, of course, that you have the right to give them, and to speak on the family's behalf." She looked at him and he glared back until she felt she was shriveling away.

"I am Carlo de Terralba, and I am head of this family. Does that satisfy you?"

"I . . . I beg your pardon."

"Not at all, Mademoiselle." He bowed, turned on his heel and walked out.

She stood there in utter confusion. But then it occurred to her that something had been achieved. After this unforeseen and extraordinary encounter she at least knew what the enemy was like. He was the personification of all she had imagined: oppression, violence, animosity and injustice. He was not approachable; nor would it be easy to outwit him; she would have to be circumspect. And yet, in an odd way, she was relieved.

It would be better than fighting the Marchesa, whom despite herself, she liked. Better, far better, if the battle were with Carlo.

BACK IN HER ROOM, that evening, she drew up a confidential report and headed it, "For the attention of Mlle Georgette Lassalle."

Arrived at Castel Terralba on September 14th, as planned, and have so far gathered the following information:

Situation. Some miles from Núoro, in mountainous, sparsely populated countryside. Very backward and remote and strikes me as unsuitable for the scheme you have in mind.

The castle itself is a fortress straight out of the Middle Ages, but the interior has been modernized to a considerable degree of comfort. The surrounding orchards, vineyards and olive groves are all part of the property, with whole families living on the land as under a feudal lord. Many actually work in the castle, for what I imagine are very low wages. Most of the servants were born here, either in the village or else nearby, and only a few of them speak proper Italian. No one but the family speaks French.

Family. First, the Dowager Marchesa de Terralba, known as *la mamma.* She is the real power and treated as such. Uses, expertly, a self-propelling wheelchair, but has all her faculties about her. A natural authoritarian, with penetrating eyes that bore right through you. The household accounts come to her and it is she who gives the cook her daily orders. Has a secretary, a Milanese girl named Alma. Alma, of course, speaks Italian and some French; talkative, and has supplied these details.

Next, the Marchesa Eleonora, the Dowager Marchesa's daughter-in-law. A widow, fiftyish, still very beautiful. The Marchese Filippo, her husband, cannot have done the kidnapping, as was thought, for he died four years ago. She comes of an old line of local land-owners who, like the Terralbas, have never moved away to the mainland, but live here on their estates in semifeudal conditions.

Thirdly, Maria Pia de Terralba, the old lady's younger daughter—Luciana's great aunt and Donna Eleonora's sister-in-law. More than forty. Has her own rooms in the castle and a staff of her own, including a sort of duenna-companion who accompanies her wherever she goes as though she were still eighteen and had to be chaperoned.

Then, the present Marchese, or Marquis as we would say in France, Carlo, younger son of the Marchesa Eleonora and uncle of Luciana. Cannot be much more than twenty-five. The only man in the family and its undisputed head, whom the women obey without question. He appears to be hot-tempered, dictatorial and proud and must, I feel, have been the kidnapper. His attitude towards Luciana's mother is hostile and vindictive.

These people are apparently much loved by their dependents. Alma tells me the villagers speak nothing but Sardinian, so I have had no contact with them, but it would be foolish to expect help or cooperation there. We shall have to rely on our own efforts.

Timetable. My whole day is spent with Luciana, and we take our meals together. Twice we have been out for a drive with Giuseppe, the porter. Donna Maria Pia came too, though whether they suspect anything and she was keeping an eye on me is difficult to say. It may well be that they suspect anyone who comes from outside their closed and secret world.

Pen in hand, Marion paused to consider what she had written. To be honest, she would feel a great deal more comfortable if they were suspicious. It was distasteful to think of betraying their trust, whereas if they had misgivings she could do what she had to do with no qualms of conscience. Or could she? None of her own arguments really reconciled her to her role, nor dispelled an overriding uneasiness. She concluded her report: Luciana, I must emphasize, is perfectly well in every way, surrounded by affection and obviously happy. This may be hard to accept, but it is the truth and I cannot disguise it.

Having added these remarks she folded the sheets of paper and put them in an envelope, together with several photographs of the castle and the countryside she had taken during the week; all useful material for Georgette Lassalle when she planned her sortie.

Then came the problem of how to send it off, for she had to see to this herself.

There was a mailbox in the courtyard, which the postman emptied almost every day, but that might not be safe. The best thing would be to send it registered mail from the post office in Núoro on her day off. But how did one get there? Núoro was too far for Giuseppe and the horses. Alma, when consulted, suggested Giovanni and the car.

"But isn't he Don Carlo's chauffeur?"

"Oh, no, he's the family chauffeur. Carlo doesn't use him much; he has an Alfa Romeo and drives himself. You'd think he was on a racetrack, too."

Marion raised an eyebrow, "That sounds a bit modern for these surroundings. Anyway, he's always on a horse when I see him. I didn't connect him with cars."

"Oh, he spends his time hunting boar and wild sheep and things just now. He adores it. He'll go back to his usual routine when the season's over—off to Macomer and Sassari and places. Leaves the horse behind."

"What does he do, then, when he isn't hunting?" enquired Marion, idly.

"Studies ancient architecture. He's discovered a village of those *nuraghi*—you know, houses or forts or whatever they are, made of enormous stones. Look like great beehives. They're all over Sardinia and people study them." Alma obviously enjoyed passing on information.

"Don Carlo's interested in that sort of thing?" Marion was surprised to hear it. It was somehow out of character.

"He adores his excavations. And he writes books about them, and articles in magazines."

"You don't mean to tell me he's an archeologist?"

"Yes, that's right. He's quite famous for it."

Marion began to laugh.

"What's so funny?" said Alma, offended.

"The picture it conjures up. He looks more like a wild barbarian than an intellectual to me."

"Goodness, he doesn't have to be middle-aged, with a beard, does he?"

"Well, that's my idea of a famous scholar, more or less."

"Then you must be very conventional," was the scornful rejoinder.

"Sorry. It's all new to me, remember—the country, the people here. I can't sort them out properly yet."

"He's fantastic, though, absolutely fantastic," continued Alma, fervently. "If only he weren't so absorbed in his beastly fossils the whole time!"

Ah, thought Marion in some amusement, *he has cast his spell on mamma's secretary.*

Changing the subject, she asked various questions about life on the island instead, and led up to what she really wanted to know. "Alma, how long have you been here at Castel Terralba."

"Me? Eight months."

But it was three years since Luciana had been kidnapped, so Alma could have known nothing about it. Had she done so, she might possibly think Carlo somewhat less fantastic.

"Did you ever meet Luciana's father?"

"Oh, no. He's been dead for a while, anyway. It was awful for them. He was the eldest son, and very promising, and everything. He was supposed to marry some local heiress, but then an adventuress got hold of him."

"Have you heard anything about her? Luciana's mother, I mean."

"Oh, no, they never mention her. Just as well, too. She came from simply nowhere and brought all that shame and scandal on them. And then she abandoned her daughter, too."

"Are you sure?"

"Luciana's here, isn't she? They're bringing her up; that proves it. Anyhow," she added blithely, "if it wasn't for that you wouldn't be here either. I bet they pay you a decent salary?"

Alma loved discussing salaries. The conversation took a financial turn and other topics were forgotten.

Chapter 7

The file sitting on M. Perdrière's desk had increased in bulk since the visit from Mlle Lassalle. In addition to the original documents, Perdrière had filed for and received several injunctions, as well as initiating proceedings on Marion Maresco's legal separation from her husband. With a purely malicious thrill, the old man gathered up the several writs he was to serve on the unsuspecting Stanislas this afternoon and placed them neatly at the top of the pile on his desk.

Maresco entered the office ten minutes later, rigid and businesslike in a perfectly tailored gray linen suit, his lean, saturnine face obviously struggling to repress a smile. Perdrière gave him several moments to compose his features, taking a perverse satisfaction in the knowledge that the predator standing before him would have no trouble looking bereaved once the writs were in his hands.

"Please be seated, Monsieur," said Perdrière at last. "I have several documents for you."

As he found the chair, Stanni began searching the the inner breast pocket of his jacket for a pen.

"Just tell me where you want me to sign," he told the lawyer.

"Oh, there is no need for your signature on these, Monsieur. All you have to do is receive them."

One by one, without a word of explanation, Perdrière handed Maresco the documents: the writ of separation; the writ notifying him of the impending sale of the perfume factory; the injunction ordering him to cease all operations within the firm; the injunction ordering a halt to the operation of the firm Maresco had set up to pirate old Maraval's chemical formulas; and a document Perdrière was especially proud of, a declaration from the *Deuxième Bureau* and the Municipal Police of Paris that until the investigation into the causes of the "plane explosion" had been completed, Maresco was not to leave town.

Once the papers had all been delivered, Perdrière sat back in his chair, smiling ingenuously, as Maresco sputtered and strangled like a drowning man. His face was slowly turning the same color as his suit. At last, he found breath to speak.

"What kind of sordid trick is this?" he demanded in a voice that was almost a shriek.

"No trick, I guarantee you, Monsieur. Marion Maraval Maresco is alive. I am in possession of certain documents," said Perdrière calmly, patting the file folder in question, "which are in perfect legal order and which prove that your wife did not die in the accident. Naturally, I have stopped the probation of her will."

Maresco sat in shocked silence for a minute or more, then licked his lips nervously and blurted out, "I want to see her, speak to her, make sure for myself that she is alive!"

"No doubt," the lawyer purred, "but as you can see from the very first document I placed in your hands, she does not wish to see you, and it is her wish that I must respect."

"Her wish that you must respect?" echoed the younger man, incredulously, leaning forward on his chiar and swaying like a cobra about to spring. "What about *my* wishes and rights? What about justice?"

"Justice is scrved equally well if the two of you do not meet," intoned Perdrière equitably. "After the shock of nearly losing her life, followed by the deeper shock of discovering your true attitude toward her, surely you can understand why she would want to be alone for a while."

Suddenly feeling very warm and uncomfortable, Maresco loosened his tie, then began leafing frantically through the official documents on his lap.

"Oh, you won't find an address there, I'm afraid," Perdrière advised him.

Maresco threw the papers down on Perdrière's desk angrily.

"Who the hell is this Georgette Lassalle?" he snapped.

"Merely a colleague of mine who has agreed to act on your wife's behalf. You won't find her address there, either."

No, thought Maresco, *but she has to have an office somewhere in Paris. It's a start.*

The younger man took several deep breaths and licked his lips again.

"I don't believe that Marion would do this to me," he said finally, choking on every word, "and I don't believe that she is alive. This is some sort of dirty trick being played by someone who wants to see me ruined, and I intend to get to the bottom of it, with or without your cooperation."

Perdrière sighed deeply. "Monsieur, you must know how unethical it would be for me to represent both sides of this dispute; therefore, I have one last piece of advice for you, before we become adversaries."

"And what is that?" snarled Maresco.

"Get yourself a good lawyer."

Perdrière watched as Maresco, his lips white with fury, scooped up the papers from the edge of the lawyer's desk and stamped out the door, without a word of goodbye. As the door slammed behind the lean, gray, ramrod-stiff figure, Monsieur Perdrière permitted himself a small, smug smile.

AS HE HEARD the doorbell ring, Maresco rushed from the study, where he had been pacing impatiently back and forth. Flinging open the front door, he grabbed his sister by the arm and yanked her inside, pausing only long enough to lock the door behind her. Carole settled herself demurely on the modern striped sofa, shrugged out of her sweater, stretched both arms out along the top edge of the cushions and said, "Well? What was this terribly urgent matter that you couldn't discuss with me over the phone and wouldn't see me at the office about?" She crossed one leg over the other and let the upper leg swing from side to side.

Maresco watched her for a moment before answering. She was the image of self-confidence, as he had been only several hours earlier, and he wanted to remember her in this pose. As Perdrière had done, Maresco dropped the documents into her lap one by one, giving her several seconds to digest the title at the top of each page before covering it with the next. First, the leg stopped swinging; then the arms came down, the legs uncrossed and Carole Jordan was sitting tensely at the edge of her seat, staring uncomprehendingly up at her brother as the brittle documents she held in shaking hands made a subdued rustling sound.

"What does this mean?" she whispered in horror.

"She's alive," he said baldly, "and she knows. She's

suing for a separation. And she's keeping me out of the factory."

Carole had seized upon one document and was scanning it with widened eyes.

"She's *selling* the factory—and all the formulas!" she exclaimed bitterly. "You're her husband—you have legal rights as long as you're married to her! Can't you talk her out of this?"

"I can't talk to her if nobody will tell me where she is!" he retorted angrily and flopped down onto the couch beside Carole. "She doesn't want to see me, according to old Perdrière, the company lawyer."

"Well, she has to see you," declared Carole firmly. "Who is this Lassalle woman?"

Maresco shrugged. "Some kind of legal proxy for Marion. Lassalle is a lawyer, with an office on Pergolèse Street."

"Have you been in touch with her?"

"I telephoned, before calling you. She's out for the rest of the day. I'm to call again tomorrow morning to make an appointment."

Carole was frowning into space thoughtfully.

"There is one angle we can cover right now," she told her brother, beginning to brighten up. "I'm going to call the firm that did the investigation for old Maraval and find out whether anyone has been in touch with them about this case. It's possible that Marion doesn't know about that report; if so, you're still relatively safe."

As Carole picked up the receiver, Maresco turned and hurried into the kitchen to fix himself a drink.

"THANK YOU, Monsieur."

With a sigh, Georgette Lassalle replaced the receiver in its cradle and stroked out the next name on her rapidly diminishing list. There was a remote possibility that Maraval had contacted a firm whose head office

was not in Paris at all, but in Marseille or in Strasbourg.
If so, that made the search triply difficult.

At the sound of the office door opening, she looked
up. It was only Pierre, the day receptionist, bringing her
another cup of coffee. Consulting her watch, Lassalle
noted mechanically that she had missed lunch
altogether.

"Thank you, Pierre," she said, taking the styrofoam
cup from his hand and sipping it gratefully. She could
only spend another hour doing this; she had an
apppointment with Paulette Arnaudy at four o'clock.
It was unfortunate that there had been such a delay in
getting Marion on the plane; otherwise, she might have
received a report by now. Arnaudy would be disap-
pointed that there was no news as yet on the status of
her little girl. Ah, well. . . .

Putting the cup down beside the three other empty
styrofoam cups on her desk, she picked up the receiver
of her telephone again. She consulted the list, then di-
aled the next number, mentally reviewing what she
was going to say to whomever answered the phone at
Bessant and Rougeon Investigations. There was naturally a great deal of jealousy in the private investigations business, especially where the Lady Detective
was concerned. Some of her colleagues, despite their
respect for the results she achieved, deplored some of
her methods, calling her a glory-grabbing super-
woman. In locating the firm that old Maraval had
hired, she had to be careful not to give the impression
that she wanted to take credit for all the careful research that had gone into their report to him, or that
she intended to use their work as a stepping-stone to
still more glory. The wording of her request had to be
just so.

The phone was answered on the fourth ring by a
female voice.

"Bessant and Rougeon," she announced sweetly.

"Good afternoon," said Lassalle, as brightly as she could, despite the fact that she'd been on the phone since ten o'clock that morning. "I am a solicitor representing Marion Maraval Maresco. At her request, I have reopened the investigation into the death of her father, Félicien Maraval. According to my information, the deceased hired a firm of private investigators shortly before his heart attack, and I am presently trying to locate that firm. Could you tell me, please, whether you have done any work in the past for Monsieur Maraval?"

There was a pause on the other end, and then the female voice said, "Perhaps you had best speak to Monsieur Bessant. One moment, please."

Georgette sighed. She had had to give that whole story to every receptionist at every firm on her list, just to speak to someone who could answer her question. And now she would have to repeat it again, carefully omitting mentioning her name unless asked point-blank who she was.

"Henri Bessant speaking." The voice was a pleasant tenor, conjuring up in Lassalle's mind an image of business suite, steel-rimmed glasses and a salesman's smile.

"Good afternoon," she began again, a trifle wearily, "I am a solicitor representing Marion Maraval Maresco—"

"Of course," broke in Bessant, "Félicien Maraval's daughter."

Lassalle felt her heart jump into her throat.

"You knew the gentleman?" she inquired diffidently.

"We had a business arrangement," said Bessant firmly, "which, naturally, being a lawyer yourself, you will understand was strictly confidential."

"Of course!" exclaimed the detective. "But I wonder whether I could come in sometime tomorrow and discuss my present case with you."

"You wish to initiate a business arrangement with us?"

"In a manner of speaking, yes," she confirmed, unspeakably relieved that the long string of telephone calls was over. "I can see you for an hour tomorrow afternoon, at three," he replied. Lassalle did a mental review of her own schedule for the next day before accepting the appointment.

"May I know with whom I have this appointment?" he asked politely.

"I would prefer not to identify myself over the phone, Monsieur."

"Ah, I see. In that case, until tomorrow at three o'clock, Madame X."

WITH A TRIUMPHANT LOOK, Carole hung up the receiver and swaggered over to the couch where her brother sat sipping a cocktail.

"I gather we're safe for the moment," he observed drily.

"Nobody has even telephoned to make inquiries," she crowed, deftly removing the drink from his hand and taking a swallow of it before giving it back. "Now, we have to take steps to find this wife of yours and talk some sense into her before she can go ahead with the sale. Have you talked to any of your friends? Perhaps they know something."

Maresco shook his head.

"Nobody has heard from her. Really, Carole, if she wanted to stay hidden from me, she wouldn't be stupid enough to talk to any of our mutual friends."

"Oh," said Carole, a little chastised. "Perhaps I have been underestimating her. Well, then, how is she living? She can't have touched any of your savings or checking accounts, and the pocket money she had for the last two weeks of your vacation must have run out by now." Maresco suddenly looked very thoughtful.

"Someone must be giving her money," he declared, causing his sister to remark sarcastically:

"Brilliant deducation, Stanni."

"You're the last person who should be passing judgment on me," he said, savagely, in a voice that belied the sad, tormented look on his face. Now that his wife had returned from the dead, he was the image of bereavement.

Chapter 8

The two women, situated somewhere between the servants and the family, came to know each other better as the days went by. Since Alma, never one to miss an opportunity, had decided to improve her French she had spent much of her abundant leisure time in Luciana's nursery schoolroom. Marion gladly welcomed her.

"I was bored stiff before you came," Alma confided. "It's not much fun being with those old girls all the time. Maria Pia's the youngest and she's well over forty. Honestly. It's just heavenly to talk to somebody of the same generation."

She was a friendly soul and might have made a useful ally, but Marion had realized from their very first exchange, that Alma belonged with the opposition. She had adopted the Terralba version of Luciana's story and it would not be safe to try to disillusion her. You could tell her that these ostensibly excellent and clean-living people had carried off a child and were keeping her from her mother, in defiance of law and common humanity; but would she perceive the implications?

Indeed Alma, a comely redhead with strongly marked features, green-flecked eyes and a perfect complexion, was hardly a deep thinker. She was a flighty, if engaging young woman who fussed continually about her appearance and dressed to great advantage. However, Marion found her refreshing and enjoyed her company. It was Alma who obtained permission for Giovanni to take the governess to Núoro tomorrow, her day off.

Núoro was a typical, unspoiled Sardinian town and well deserved a visit. Marion had stayed there the night of her arrival, but there had been no time to explore it then, and now she had other things to do. First she wanted to go to the post office, and after that to meet a contact of Georgette Lassalle. This was the man who had helped with the original inquiries into the kidnapping, and thanks to him the Parisian investigator had known that a nursery-governess was wanted at the castle. Marion knew she would have to do these two things with care and caution.

This being so, she was anything but pleased when Alma announced that evening that she had also arranged to have the day off and was coming too. But since Marion could not change the arrangements, she made the best of it, said she was delighted and privately resolved to shed her companion in the course of the day.

Alma was in raptures at the prospect. "Oh, I am really looking forward to it! Just think, we won't have aunt Maria Pia around, for a change. Unless she decides to join us, of course. You can't move a yard outside this palace without her tagging along."

Heavens, not that as well, thought Marion in desperation. *How could one possibly evade the watchful eye of these punctilious Sardinians?*

But when faced with the prospect of rising at dawn for the sake of a tiring drive on mountain roads and a day spent trailing about Núoro, complete with escort, Maria Pia preferred to stay in bed. If it had been Cagliari, now, or Sassari, tourist places with lots of modern buildings and nice shops and something going on, she might have been tempted; but Núoro was nothing but old streets.

Poor Maria Pia led a very dull life as an unmarried daughter, imprisoned by custom and tradition behind the family battlements at home. She did not enjoy it at all, and there was no good reason why it should not continue, just as it was, forever.

Marion and Alma crossed the wide courtyard like children leaving school. The Fiat stood waiting under its striped awning, but Giovanni was as yet nowhere in sight. Then a horn sounded, an Alfa Romeo emerged from the garage and Carlo leaned out.

"Good morning!" he said. "May I give you a lift, or do I go too fast for you?"

"Oh no, Signore, no," cried Alma, in a flutter. "Would you take us, really?"

"With the greatest pleasure."

"That's absolutely marvelous!" For Alma, the day was made.

Carlo emerged from the car. He wore a light blue, polo-necked shirt that went very well with his tan. He was smiling and polite and looked younger than Marion had thought him at their previous meeting.

"I have to go to Núoro, as it happens," he said, "so we needn't trouble Giovanni. And I can promise you'll get there sooner."

This suggestion upset Marion's program altogether. "I don't feel like breaking my neck," she objected.

"Nervous?" He shot an amused glance in her direction.

"Yes, I am rather. I'm not awfully fond of speed."

"Oh, I love it!" Alma was all fire and mettle. "It's so thrilling."

"You don't have to worry," said Carlo to Marion. "One doesn't exactly break records on these roads, you know, and we're only on the highway for a mile or two. Come on."

Alma was in the front seat already, face alight, green eyes shining, gazing at Carlo in open adoration. Marion got in the back seat, more than a little annoyed and feeling that the other, with her animated chatter, was not behaving very well. Carlo himself appeared to take no notice. As they drove, however, Marion forgot everything save the grandeur of the surroundings, for this was the Barbagia, the wild heart of the island. Past Macomer the lonely road wound up by scattered farms to Núoro; a cold wind blew from the high peaks and Monte Ortobene rose before them. It was a country of *nuraghi*, those fortified dwelling places built in Sardinia long ago whose dark conical shapes stood in stony clearings on either side of the road.

The landscape was awe-inspiring, with a mysterious magic of its own, and her anxieties diminished in its presence. Even the feather-headed Alma fell silent, perhaps because Carlo had ceased entirely to respond, only turning to his other passenger from time to time with some interesting detail or to point something out as they passed.

Absorbed in what she saw, Marion asked him questions and he answered with enthusiasm, evidently pleased that this foreigner was so quickly stirred by the history and customs of his country and that she made such sensible and appreciative observations.

Marion liked archeology, though she had never studied it. The Sicilian holidays of her childhood had implanted a taste for classical temples and sightseeing generally, and she had been to Greece.

Once, too, her father took her to Mexico, where he

wanted to see the Mayan and Aztec remains, so she was acquainted with the subject and could discuss it intelligently. The result—though she would never have gone out of her way to achieve it—was a friendlier feeling between herself and Carlo. For the moment she forgot he was the man who had stolen Luciana. They spoke of the passing scenery while Alma sat yawning in her corner at such an impossible conversation.

They came to the new scenic highway cut out of the mountainside, and the panorama was stupendous. Gigantic, jumbled, like a vision of judgment day, the limestone hills to the south stood in glittering contrast to the noble granite peaks of the northern range, their flanks dark with huge oak forests that soared into the brilliant blue. Then from among its terraces, Núoro came into view, watched over by an enormous statue of Christ higher up the mountain.

They stopped just inside the town and Alma and Marion, dizzy from the ride, alighted. Alma wanted to visit the hairdresser and go shopping; Carlo had business of his own; and Marion merely said she had "things to do." Greatly to her relief they separated, after arranging to meet late in the afternoon.

It was market day and couples, perched on small Sardinian mounts, came riding in, the women in wide spreading skirts that covered most of the animals' backs as they sat, astride, behind their men. In spite of some modern concrete constructions—for the 'developers' had arrived some years ago—the old center still kept its village atmosphere. Life and affairs revolved around the Croso Garibaldi, where men concluded deals over their glasses of local wine amid such a crowd that Marion could hardly force her way through to the post office. Yet once she had left that area behind the streets and squares were comparatively lifeless in the blinding light.

In one of the concrete blocks, she found the address

that Georgette Lassalle had given her and asked for
Signore Petrucci. He was away, but his wife received
her in an up-to-date office on the third floor. Marion
left a message to say there was nothing to add to the
report that had gone to Paris and that she awaited further instructions.

She stepped outside again and was soon back into
another age. In a square through which she passed, the
women, all in black, came to the fountain for water and
carried away their filled jars balanced on their heads.
Ragged children played in the sun, and sheltered from
the dust and heat; old men with withered faces and
dark, bright eyes sat on their heels in the depths of
massive stone doorways. Gazing from under bushy
brows at some distant inner vision they seemed not to
see her as she passed.

She had eaten at a small restaurant—a slice of the
famous smoked ham of the region and bread from a
wondrously shaped Sardinian loaf, with a big glass of
white wine to wash it down.

She remembered having seen a chapel on the Ortobene road just beyond the town. Would Alma, she
wondered, have recognized its style as Pisan Roman-
esque? And what was it called? The Solitudine, Our
Lady of Solitude? A little striped building, whose alter-
nating bands of white limestone and black basalt
blended harmoniously in typical Sardinian contrast.
She would go there and rest.

Inside, the Solitudine was full of soft, diffused light.
She sat in a chair and let the quiet of the deserted place
wash through her in a bittersweet flood. Recently she
had been able to distract her mind, but her own misery
was still there, unchanged, waiting to spring; and here,
in the empty chapel, it took her by the throat.

The anesthetic of the past few weeks wore off. She
thought once more of how her father died, leaving her
to be flung into that swamp of lying and hypocrisy,

there to live in ignorance of the truth about her life. And now, irreparably hurt, without support or protection, she was lost and alone in a foreign country, faced with a task that was beyond her. The tears came pouring down as they had done that first night, when she had been by herself.

There was a touch on her shoulder and a low voice said, "What's the matter?"

Carlo was kneeling beside her, speaking gently, looking anxious. Horrified, she dabbed at her eyes with a handkerchief and pressed her hands to her cheeks, thankful that the dim light would help to hide the tear stains.

"Nothing's the matter. I've had a bit too much sun, that's all; I'm not used to it yet."

"Oh, yes; so you have."

He said no more but rose and waited at the end of the row of chairs as she, too, rose to her feet.

"Did you come to pray to the Virgin?" Now the words were tinged with irony.

"Did you?"

"I? Perhaps. In any case, it's pleasant in here, out of the heat."

They were whispering, though there was nobody to hear them, standing in the feeble light of the candle flames.

"Well, have you finished?"

"Yes," she said, curtly.

"May I take you to the car, then?"

She followed him into the intense sunlight, pausing to admire the facade with its rough stone figures and inspect the small columns with their carved capitals. He watched her as she examined it carefully.

"This is one of my favorite churches," he said. "I come up here whenever I'm in Núoro. Grazia Deledda is buried here, did you know?"

"The novelist?"

"That's right. Her books are about Sardinia. Have you read them?"

"I'm afraid not. But didn't she receive a Nobel Prize for literature?"

"Long before you were born, yes. Before I was born, too, to come right down to it. They're wonderful books. Nobody ever delved inside the Sardinian character as she did, nor described the island half so well. And she's still worth reading, after forty years."

Clearly these books meant a great deal to him, for the deep voice shook a little as he spoke of them.

They were walking side by side along a narrow street. The donkeys trotted home with their masters from market, and shepherds went by in their big round capes, their *berrette* on their heads.

"And did Grazia Deledda get inside the violence and savagery too?" she asked suddenly, staring straight ahead of her.

"What is that supposed to mean?" His face was expressionless.

"One hears so many stories of bandits in Sardinia."

He smiled pityingly. "Folklore, that's all. Legends."

"One hears," she persisted, still looking away from him, "that Sardinians have very little respect for the law; that they go in for armed robbery. Kidnapping, even."

He replied as calmly as before, with a slight shrug, "What an absurd notion. You must be confusing banditry with the vendetta."

"I thought that was only in Corsica?"

"No, we and the Corsicans see eye to eye on anything to do with honor, family honor, especially. We manage to be both sophisticated and primitive, I suppose, and our feelings are deep. We cherish our independence; friendship is sacred to us; a guest is sacred; we stand by our given word. But Corsicans and Sardinians are also very proud. If we think anyone has humiliated us, hatred takes over. An insult must be avenged in blood; nothing else will do."

"But we're in the twentieth century! That isn't a civilized way to live."

"I never said we were civilized," was the cold reply. "That is possibly why we don't merge with western Europe terribly well. We may have our airports and hotels with swimming pools, and investment property, and money flowing into the tourist industry, but Sardinia doesn't change. We are still savage and secret. I am happy to say," he added, after a brief pause.

"So it must always be violence," she said bitterly. "Justice taken into your own hands?"

"Justice left to itself can be a distressingly slow process; the real culprit sometimes goes scot-free. A Sardinian would never stand for that. He takes care of his own revenge and every member of his family helps him. That is our tradition."

"It's barbarous."

"If someone who brings sorrow and suffering to others expects to go on afterwards as though nothing were wrong, that is shameful." His words rasped. "Whoever is to blame must pay."

"But to be implacable like that is medieval. I couldn't agree with it, ever."

"No, well, I imagine the western mind can't understand these things." His voice was normal again, as if he had dismissed the subject.

They had reached the car. On a wall, waiting, sat Alma, plainly annoyed. Her auburn hair was newly done and her arms were full of packages. She mustered up a strained smile at their approach.

"At last! I can't tell you how tired I am. I've been around every store in the place."

As Carlo put her parcels in the trunk she regarded Marion with mistrust. "Did you make a date with him, or something?"

"Don't be so silly. We met in the Solitudine chapel; absolute coincidence."

But Alma was not to be comforted and took hasty possession of the front seat as though in the teeth of dangerous opposition.

Oh, now she's jealous, thought Marion, startled and amused at the same time. It would have set Alma's heart at rest to know that Marion in fact disliked him, and that her reasons for coming to the castle would hardly win Carlo's heart.

Yet he had his attractions, she could quite see that, and a girl of Alma's type would be susceptible. But Marion happened to know something about attractive men. She had believed Stanni to possess every virtue and good quality; had gone on believing it for the best part of two more or less intimate years. No, with men you must be wary, always. Experience has proven that, and the proof had brought her life crashing around her.

Alma gazed fiercely at Carlo's profile all the way back to the castle, ceasing this unnerving scrutiny only to cast triumphant glances over her shoulder at Marion as she sat quietly in the back seat.

Was that the way Marion had gazed at Stanni during those halcyon two years; possessively, passionately, resenting every other woman who attracted his attention? No, she finally decided, her English education had bred that kind of openness out of her. She had still felt the possessiveness, the passion, and some pride that, of all the girls who had crossed his path, Stanni had chosen to marry *her*. But to advertise those feelings would have gone contrary to what she had been taught was seemly. Her pride had taken quieter, more ladylike forms.

From the moment that they were man and wife, Marion had refused to take off her wedding ring, no matter what. Whenever she and Stanni were out in public together, everyone knew that this man was spoken for. And in the circles in which they had moved, that was all the warning necessary.

How proud she had been when Stanni had chosen her to share his life, how totally oblivious to the many things he had simply taken from her in return! Her mouth twisted derisively as the list grew in her mind: Stanni controlled the money, her father's company, the home they had chosen together. Why, she hadn't even dared to pick up her clothes. Every stitch in her suitcase had belonged to poor Florence Montagne.

Stanislas Maresco had, in acquiring Marion as his wife, also acquired the legal right to turn her out of her own home, to do her out of her own inheritance, to send her away with nothing but the clothes on her back. Marion's only hope for freedom and—yes, let's call it by its name—revenge lay in dissolving the marriage, for with it went Stanni's rights. Maybe someday, the laws would change in France, and a wife would have some form of redress against the husband who cheated her.

Coming back to the present, Marion realized suddenly that she had been gazing mindlessly at Alma's ear for heaven knew how many minutes. The Alfa Romeo was turning in at the gate to the castle. Alma cast one last glance over her shoulder and was visibly upset to find Marion smiling amicably at her, seeming not the least bit disturbed by Alma's display of puppy love.

Chapter 9

"Now what is it?" demanded Carole Jordan impatiently. She was on the phone at the offices of Maraval Perfumes, where Stanni had been telephoning her several times daily, much to her annoyance. She could understand why he was doing it, of course. That injunction had kept him from getting past the guard at the front gate for a couple of weeks now, and he was curious about what was going on inside. The poor man couldn't even continue his own projects on the side, hinging as they did on his thefts, one by one, of the Maraval formulas and patents, also protected by an injunction.

It was only a matter of time until something would evict him from the house in la Celle Saint-Cloud; until then, he was reduced to pacing like a caged animal, while the levels of his liquor bottles went down and the bills kept mounting up. Thank Heaven that Carole had managed to keep her job, at least. She was able to help him out from time to time, now that Perdrière had delivered the injunction that froze all the couple's joint assets until the marriage issue was settled. Stanni couldn't even withdraw pocket money from the bank.

"I finally have an appointment with Georgette Lassalle!" exclaimed Maresco.

Carole gazed skyward, visibly unimpressed. "And after only two weeks!" she remarked. "How wonderful that she will consent to see you, at last!"

"Well, what else could I do?" he muttered. "If I could get at our savings, I could hire a private investigator to watch her, but I'm broke. Paying a retainer to that fancy lawyer you dug up for me cleaned out my personal assets, and everything else of mine is tied up in that little factory."

Carole sighed.

"As it turns out," she pointed out relentlessly, "you couldn't get an investigator to keep an eye on Lassalle. I know, because I tried. Georgette Lassalle is called the Lady Detective, and her colleagues respect her too much to take on the job, no matter what money is being offered. They simply won't do it."

"But Perdrière—"

"Perdrière is another story altogether," she interrupted him. "My people have been watching him for nearly a week."

"And . . . ?" he asked eagerly.

"And nothing," she spat. "A waste of time. The man hasn't altered his routine one iota in all that time. He hasn't been seen dropping off packages, or even mailing letters. And the only people he speaks to are those who wouldn't know Marion if they tripped over her. So it isn't Perdrière who's been supporting your flyaway spouse."

"Please, Carole," he begged her, "don't be flippant."

"I'm not being flippant," she barked at him. "Do you think I enjoy coming up against these brick walls? Do you think my resources are limitless? That week's surveillance cost me two weeks' salary! I should have had a raise by now, but I've been too scared to ask for it—how do you think I enjoy *that*?"

On the other end of the line, there was only silence. Maresco could appreciate very well the agony of restlessness his sister was going through. Never before had one person posed such insurmountable barriers to them both at once. Always, when one had failed, the other could bring off some measure of success; but Marion's disappearance, compounded by the various injunctions brought against him, had stymied them both. And the tension of waiting for the other shoe to fall was slowly but surely eroding their own relationship, as they snapped and snarled at each other like wolves caged side by side.

"How is the sale proceeding?" he asked humbly after a moment's silence.

"Remarkably well," she said flatly, and left it at that. Maresco knew that Perdrière had been parading prospective buyers through the plant since the day of their meeting, two long weeks ago. Much of the equipment in the factory had already been sold in lots to the various perfumeries in the city; there was only the shell of the building itself, as well as the office furnishings, to dispose of now. Maresco knew, as well, that Perdrière was selling all the Maraval patents, which made him even jumpier than before.

After all, a wife couldn't sue her husband for taking her inherited patents and setting up in business for himself; but once the patents were sold to other, larger interests, then Maresco was leaving himself open to criminal charges the moment any of his stolen perfumes hit the market. And the injunction was effectively preventing him from marketing any of them before the sale went through. Perdrière had taken pains to see to it that Stanislas Maresco wouldn't make a penny's profit from his misdeeds.

THE WOMAN SEATED opposite Georgette Lassalle had thick wavy brown hair and a deep, melodious voice. Draped carelessly over her shoulders was a stole of pastel mink. Her lips were very red, and her skin was pale; and in the stark pristine whiteness of Lassalle's office, she looked sensational. But it was not her looks that interested the women at that moment.

"I have had a report from my agent in Sardinia," said Lassalle, patting a voluminous file folder.

"And is it favorable?" demanded Paulette Arnaudy.

"It is . . . ambivalent."

"What?!" said the client sharply, with an abrupt intake of breath.

"The situation is not as well defined as we have all been led to believe," Georgette Lassalle told her calmly, ignoring the sudden flushing of her client's cheeks.

"Which means exactly what?"

"While it is true that the Terralba family, out of context, can be as austere and unbending as you indicated to me, it seems that they love Luciana—Lucy—very much and are providing a warm and loving home atmosphere for her. She is far from unhappy with them."

"How can she be? They hate me!"

"So my contact informs me. But children have very short memories. And they do not carry grudges. Given love, Lucy will love in return. And the Terralbas have been giving her love, for almost three years now."

Tears welled up in the eyes of the singer.

"Mademoiselle Lassalle, I must have her back! As soon as possible!"

"I can understand your desire for haste, Madame," the detective reassured her, "but it is precisely now, now when we have someone inside the family situation, that we must be patient. We cannot make plans without accurate information, the sort of data that takes time to gather. Before we can act my agent must be left alone to get the information we need. But once we have that information, you have my personal guarantee that no time will be wasted."

"Before Christmas?" asked the singer in a little-girl voice. "I want her to have a real, French Christmas at home, with me."

Lassalle nodded, smiling indulgently.

"I have every hope, Madame," she assured Paulette Arnaudy.

When the singer had actually swept out the door of the office, Lassalle sighed and extracted a second file folder from her desk drawer, this one marked "Maresco." Her interview with Henri Bessant had been a resounding success. He had recognized her the moment she stepped through the door of his office, had gallantly offered her a seat, and, at her request, had opened the files on Maraval Perfumes for her inspection.

The copy of their file on Stanislas Maresco had arrived at Georgette's office that very morning, about ten minutes before her appointment with Mme Arnaudy, and so she had only had time to give the material in the folder a cursory glance. Now, alone with her thoughts for several hours, she set out to peruse in detail the contents of the report that had, according to her sources, hastened Félicien Maraval to his grave. As she read, the detective became more and more deeply engrossed in the life story of Maresco, who could, she was sure, have sold his memoirs to some publisher for a fortune.

When she had turned the last page of the file, Lassalle wore a very satisfied smile. She hadn't expected a marital case to be so open-and-shut as this one was turning out to be. Yes, it would be extremely easy to get Marion what she wanted, once this rogue Maresco and

his infamous sister were confronted with the facts of
the situation.

"Poor Dora," she muttered, picking up the phone and
dialing the number of M. Perdrière's office.

Chapter 10

Attention Georgette Lassalle. Information gathered during the past three weeks.

As I become more and more a part of the family here, my position becomes increasingly delicate. Everyone is extremely kind; I am treated as one of the family. Luciana is a darling, always lively, never sulks. She has taken a fancy to me and we get along perfectly. Her great-grandmother, her great-aunt and her grandmother all spoil her, of course, and obviously she would miss them; though I think that any problems will be sorted out once she is with her mother again.

Her uncle, the original kidnapper, seems very fond of her too. It would therefore be wise to choose a time when he is away. Don Carlo is a danger for the very reason that his opinions and beliefs are genuine and sincerely held. He would not stop at violence to defend what he personally regards as right and just.

In character he is not unlike this country itself, a combination of the harsh and the sensitive. He is also, incidentally, an archeologist of repute and digs for pre-

historic remains. The other day he took me to visit a site
in the neighboring area, an ancient village he discovered and is now excavating. He has found temples and
some houses, almost untouched, with cooking utensils
and weapons. It is absolutely fascinating. He is writing
a book on the subject and should be going to Rome quite
soon, to see a publisher. This might fit in with our plans.

Having reached this point, Marion stopped to consider what those plans were. As she grew ever more
reluctant, they seemed to her every day less feasible. In
a vulnerable moment she had agreed to come here but
nothing was as she had thought it would be. Lassalle
had somehow led her to expect a sad waif pining at
Terralba, even ill-treated by hard-faced relatives. And
here was Luciana, cheerful as a sunbeam, glowing with
health and good spirits. She was much too young to
miss her mother, or to know she was deprived of the
dearest and most natural love of all. But facts were
facts; the child would undoubtedly suffer if she were
separated from her father's kin. No, some more hu-
mane solution, such as a reconciliation between the
two sides, would be far better. Yet this was scarcely to
be hoped for, given the attitude of the entire Terralba
family to Paulette Arnaudy. That unhappy woman
could do nothing but take back, by force or stratagem,
what they had stolen from her. And Marion was supposed to organize the operation.

She was about to continue the memorandum when
there was a knock on her door. She pushed the papers
into the drawer of the desk and called, "Come in."

It was Alma, slightly embarrassed and unusually
hesitant. "Am I disturbing you?"

"Of course not. Come and sit down."

"I saw Luciana was with her grandmother, so I
thought I might catch you by yourself. I wanted to talk
to you for a minute. You know they've invited us both
to this affair tomorrow?"

"Oh, yes— mamma's birthday. It'll be quite an occasion, from what I gather."

"Are you going?"

Marion looked up in astonishment. "Of course I'm going. I can't very well do anything else, can I? I'll enjoy it, in any case. It will be marvelous to see the costumes, and there'll be songs and dancing."

"Oh, yes; I suppose so." There was a pause. "What are you wearing?"

Another curious question.

"I didn't bring an enormous wardrobe with me, if that's what you mean; there isn't much to choose from. What do you want to know for?" she added, suppressing a smile.

"Do you mind if I smoke?"

"Please do."

Alma offered her a cigarette. "American ones, if you like them."

Marion took a cigarette.

Nervously, Alma lit it for her. She was evidently jumpy about something and her listener waited to see what it might be.

"I'm going to be frank." She hesitated a little, searching for the idiomatic phrase in French. "That is, I'm going to put all my cards on the table."

"But I thought you were always frank," said Marion.

"Well, if you don't mind, I would like to tell you a secret."

"That's very nice of you. I'm honored."

"Wait until you hear what it is first," said Alma, darkly. "I want you to know, I'm in love with Carlo." She sat back with the air of one who has hurled a bomb, or formally thrown down the gauntlet.

"Yes, I rather thought you might be," said Marion, as earnestly as she could.

"Well?"

"Well what? I sincerely hope he feels the same way about you."

Above the green eyes, the red gold brows drew together in a doubtful frown. Alma bit her lip. "You mean that? Honestly?"

"I wouldn't say so if I didn't. And I can't for the life of me see where I come in at all."

The Italian girl puffed furiously at her cigarette, then stubbed it out in the ashtray. "You really, honestly mean you're not interested in him?"

"Me? Good heavens no. What a thought!" Marion laughed aloud, so spontaneously and with such unmistakable astonishment that Alma was immediately reassured.

"Thank God for that," she exclaimed in relief. "I needn't worry any more."

Then she, too, laughed, though with a shade of anxiety still. There was a second's irresolute silence, which Marion broke by demanding, "Where on earth did you get that idea, may I ask? That I could possibly think of Carlo in the way that you do?"

"Oh, it's been this last day or two. Ever since we want to Núoro, actually. You seem to be getting on with him so much better. I mean, really better. Before, you just ignored him; I thought you didn't even like him. And avoiding him all the time. Yes you did— I noticed. Like never coming down to the drawing room in the evening, when you knew they expected you, as well as me."

Vaguely annoyed, Marion prevaricated. "There was Luciana to see to."

"Francesca puts her to bed."

"Well, I had my letters to write."

"But you write your letters after lunch now, and you're never out of the drawing room. You were there for hours last night, talking away to Carlo all the time and turning over music for him. I could see you."

"What about it?"

Alma nearly choked. "And there I was, trapped into playing dominoes," she hissed, through set teeth. "Maria Pia's damned everlasting dominoes!"

"But Carlo likes playing the piano, and he was playing something I enjoyed—I adore those czardas tunes. We were discussing music."

This was too much. "Oh, yes, you discuss music, and you discuss architecture and you go on about books! He never talks to anyone else about things like that. How ever did he manage before you came along, for goodness' sake?"

"I should have thought he talked to you."

"Me. Oh!" She gesticulated angrily. "What would he talk to me about? I'm not bright, like you are. Movies, pop songs, fashions, and new shows; that's what I can talk about. Things he hates. All he likes is classical music and old statues. And I loathe them—ruins and places people lived in ages ago and tombs and temples and everything. And those revenge stories, and bandits in the maquis—well, they're all right for tourists, and you seem to enjoy them, but I think they're silly.

"And I love him, really. He looks so aristocratic and proud, as if he owned the earth. And on a horse! Have you ever watched him training a horse? He was breaking one in when I first came here and honestly, once I'd seen him, I couldn't think about anything else."

She shook her auburn head. "He just has to like me. I don't think he bothers much with girl friends. Anyway, he's never brought one home. All that trouble with Luciana's parents must have put him off. And I don't see why he shouldn't notice me, sooner or later. I'm not exactly repulsive. Or so I've been told," she added, with artless vanity. "But since you came he never even looks at me."

"He never looks at me either," replied Marion, emphatically, "not in the way you mean, that is."

"I wish I could believe you." Alma's face clouded. "Then I might have a bit of a chance."

This was becoming awkward, yet Marion had no idea of how to stop the conversation. If only, she thought once more, she could explain what brought her here; if only Alma could realize how far she was from setting herself up as a rival. Determined at least to make the position clear, she laid a friendly hand on the other's wrist.

"Now, there's nothing to worry about, and that is the plain truth. Even if he was interested in me—and I can't see why he ever should be—I couldn't possibly be interested in him."

"You couldn't?" Alma found this stupifying. "Don't you like him?"

"No," said Marion, bleakly.

"You *can't* not!"

"Well, that just shows what different tastes we have. But, quite apart from that, I'm not free."

"You're in love with somebody else? Is it somebody in France? Are you engaged, or something?"

The questions poured out. Alma was herself again.

"Don't let's talk about me," Marion said firmly. "All I wanted to do was set your mind at rest. There could never be anything between your Don Carlo and me; nothing at all. I came here because I was going through a bad time in my life and I wanted a job. When I leave, I shall never see or hear of the Terralba family again. Please believe me."

She spoke with such sincerity, weighing every word, that Alma was at once restored. "Oh, yes, I believe you!" she cried, flung her arms around Marion's neck, embraced her warmly and tripped gladly away, at peace with the world.

Watching her go, Marion wished she could be as carefree as the auburn head skipping out the doorway. How easy life would be if all her problems could be summed up, as Alma's were, and confined to one spot, geographically and psychologically!

But try as she might, Marion could never seem to push Paris completely out of her mind, especially since her doubts had formed over Lassalle's plan to regain custody of the child. There was so much of herself invested in the happiness of Luciana, and she was so trusted by the family that Marion was beginning to feel like the snake in the Garden of Eden.

Like a Carole Jordan, Marion had insinuated herself into the Terralba family with ulterior motives at heart, with a purpose that could not avoid hurting someone. Unlike Carole, Marion had a conscience, one that had begun nagging at her. She realized that, contrary to what she had been told, removing the child from these surroundings would destroy her happiness, not restore it.

And now she found herself envying Alma, for whom life was a simple, linear parade of fashions, songs and infatuations. There was surely something to be said for the sheltered way of life of Italian women, and yet. . . .

How real was an emotion that ignored the happiness of the one loved? Alma had stood before Marion not two minutes before, declaring her loathing for everything that mattered to Carlo, and then in the same breath had stated that she loved him. In an adolescent approaching womanhood, that might seem a charming contradiction, but if Alma was serious, if she truly wanted Carlo for her own, such an attitude would doom the entire affair. Alma would have to grow up in a hurry, would have to realize that a man as vital, as well read, as eclectic as Carlo could strangle in the circle of her clinging arms.

Suddenly, her envy melted away, and a sort of passive pity took its place. Marion would never knowingly wish to be that young again, nor to stay that young as long as Alma had.

GEORGETTE LASSALLE LOOKED UP, an open, inviting smile on her face, as Pierre ushered the lean, ashen-faced man into her office. A little startled by the stark-ness of the decor, Stanni stood in the center of the room, trying to accustom himself to the contrasts in the office.

"So you are Stanislas Maresco!" she declared ingenu-ously, feigning delight at making his acquaintance. He smiled faintly and shook her extended hand with ob-vious lack of enthusiasm.

"And you are the elusive Georgette Lassalle," he remarked sardonically.

"Perhaps," she conceded, "you see me as elusive. It's unfortunate that my schedule has not permitted us to talk before now. If I had realized you would find com-municating with Monsieur Perdrière insufficient, I would have planned an interview with you."

"I want to see my wife," he grated. "Perdrière tells me that you are her proxy in these transactions . . . ?"

"Yes, I am. I have power of attorney, which means I can sign her name to official documents." Lassalle knew that he wanted to hear more, much more, but fell silent, with such a candid and friendly expression that doubt began to darken Maresco's features.

"Do you know where she is?" he asked finally.

"Not at this moment, no," she replied. "Madame Maresco came to this office to give me the power of attorney and to sign some papers, but that was weeks ago. I have no idea where she is now."

Maresco stood halfway up from his seat, his brow furrowed in rage.

"You must know!" he thundered. "You must be sending her reports on the progress of the case, and that means that you have an address. Even if it's only a post-office drop, *I want that address!*"

Sighing deeply, Lassalle reached into her desk drawer, an action that froze Maresco in midgesture.

Was she conceding so easily? Was this obstacle falling, like the wall around Jericho, at a single trumpet blast?

Without saying a word, Lassalle laid two pieces of paper before him on the desk. One was a letter from a Doctor Strauss, attesting to the extreme agitation of Mme Maresco's nerves; the other was a signed declaration from Marion herself, stating that she wanted to be left entirely alone, and that all reports were to be kept for her by Mlle Lassalle until such time as she indicated, by mail, that she was ready to receive them.

Stunned, Maresco looked up blankly at Lassalle, whose face still registered the same candor and certainty as before.

"When . . . " he stammered. Lassalle only shrugged.

"I have a file folder two inches thick of reports," she told him. "When she is ready, she'll let me know. And then, Monsieur, I'll be able to let you know, but not before, obviously."

Another obstacle! Rigid with fury, Maresco rose from his chair and stalked out of Lassalle's office. She smiled at his back for several seconds, and then, when it was certain that he would not return to ask one last question, she relaxed for the first time since he had entered the door. Gathering up the two documents on the desk, she added them to the file folder that emerged from a lower drawer of her filing cabinet.

The file marked "Maresco" was two inches thick by now—she had not lied about that. Scanning its contents, Lassalle did some rapid figuring in her head and came to the conclusion that it was time to begin legal proceedings for the separation.

Georgette Lassalle had not lied about one other thing—Marion really had told her, by mail, that she did not want to be bothered with the details of the affair. Cast as the villain in the drama being enacted in Sardinia, Marion was having a hard-enough time coping

with one complicated moral issue, without the sordid
details of the second situation reaching her.

Hence all their correspondence concerned the progress of the Arnaudy case. Marion's letters were always full of personal information about the members
of the Terralba family, information gleaned from dis-
cussions with Alma, usually, and were peppered with
doubt as to the moral rightness of what they were con-
templating. Lassalle's communiqués carried a great
deal of encouragement, messages from the anguished
mother of the abducted child and descriptions of the
gradual breakdown in that woman's composure as she
waited to be reunited with her child again.

Needless to say, the letters themselves were explo-
sive. If any member of the family ever opened and read
one, even by accident, the whole game would be up;
therefore, on days when the mail arrived, Marion always rushed down to meet the letter carrier, in order to
be the only one who ever saw or touched her letters.
Anyone who noticed her behavior managed to shrug it
off—the governess had a gentleman, perhaps; anyone,
that is, but a certain auburn-haired secretary who
made a habit of watching Marion's headlong dash to
the front gate to collect the mail.

MONSIEUR PERDRIÈRE STOOD behind his desk to shake
hands with Mlle Lassalle as she came in. Noting her
rosy cheeks, he commented, "The air is quite brisk
these days, Mademoiselle."

Lassalle paused in the act of opening her briefcase to
reply, "Indeed it is, Monsieur. And if there were better
parking facilities in this street, I would not have to
sample so much of it."

A Gallic shrug was his only response.

"Has everything been initiated?" she asked, when
the thick file folder was in the old man's hands and she
was seated comfortably beside him.

"Everything," he answered, smiling with satisfaction. "Although I expect that this will all be settled out of court, I have placed us on the courtroom calendar for the middle of December. Magistrate Verlaine is prepared to give us a private hearing with two weeks notice, in the matter of the divorce."

"Has he been warned of the circumstances?"

"Of the proxy? Yes—and under these conditions he is quite agreeable."

"Excellent!" Lassalle said with a genuine smile of pleasure that all was proceeding so smoothly.

"Now, what is all this?" he inquired, rifling through the pages in the folder in front of him.

"Evidence for the criminal proceedings, in case they become necessary. We should both be completely informed, since there is a possibility that I shall have to be absent during the month of December."

"Oh?" The old man raised both eyebrows.

"Another case, one that I have been working on for several years now. The timing is crucial. And, since all I could do at the trial would be to present depositions made by my client, my presence in the court is not, strictly speaking, necessary."

Perdrière could not disguise his disappointment.

"I understand, of course, Mademoiselle," he said sadly, "but I was hoping to share this victory."

Chapter 11

The first sign of the festa was the cheerful noise of a cavalcade approaching from the village. Marion, for whom the day was to mean more than she could ever have imagined, stood at her window to watch the procession coming. In a stream of life and color gaily dressed women rode pillion behind the men on horseback; others proceeded on foot in the fine-embroidered costumes they kept so carefully stored away among sachets of mint and jasmine and brought out for celebrations; draft-oxen pulled carts, paper flowers and oranges decorating their horns; flute players danced lightly through the streets; and, driven by an excited troop of children, tiny donkeys in small flowered hats capered by.

The bells rang for mass. Every week the family, their staff and the villagers worshipped in the tiny church attached to the castle itself. On this particular morning its lime-washed walls were almost invisible beneath the load of decoration; hangings and wreaths and pennons and garlands were festooned everywhere. The chapel was packed to the doors, with an overflow crowd outside.

Donna Eleonora wore the traditional gala dress of the region, a deep red velvet gown with a pointed bodice; with a lace mantilla on her head and the white streak shining in her dark hair, she was a figure of striking beauty. The old Dowager Marchesa sat enthroned in an armchair between her grandson and her daughter Maria Pia, both in Sardinian costume, Carlo with full-sleeved white shirt, buttons of gold at the cuffs and throat, a wide belt, richly embroidered, and high leggings of *orbace*, the woolen cloth woven by the women of the island.

How real and alive it all is, thought Marion. There was not the faintest suggestion of tourist-oriented folk-lore. No one wore fancy dress; they were merely Sardinians in their natural element. Their clothes and their whole appearance blended with the surroundings, magnificently right. Nothing had been dreamed up for the occasion; everything here was part of a living tradition, past and present linked in one continuous chain. These dresses were family heirlooms, worn by the women on festa days only; passed from mother to daughter, in those poor stone cottages. The jewels were handed down and treasured intact in their wrappings of fragile tissue paper, from one needy generation to another. Nobody seemed to mind being photographed and Marion wandered among them with her camera. And they were all, she found, friendly people, though very few of them understood Italian and she had to fall back on the language of smiles and gestures.

The gates of the castle stood wide open and in the courtyard a huge table was set with delicious-looking food and wine in earthenware jars. Around it surged peasants, servants, shepherds and children, mingling together in holiday joy.

After mass the heroine of the day appeared with her

entourage and the crowd rushed forward with its gifts.
The people had brought big rush-work platters and
materials of their own weaving, baskets of figs and
vegetables, dishes of fruit, pine-kernel biscuits, flat
loaves of bread, pastries made of honey and simple
bunches of paper flowers. Some of her shepherds carried young lambs on their shoulders.

Once more, Marion had the impression of moving
back in time, into another age. She was bewildered by
this patriarchal atmosphere, as though she were in a
strange and different world, at the heart of something
that had not changed for centuries. She felt wrong and
out of place. And when she remembered what had
brought her there in the first place, she felt more alien
than ever.

Alma, unseen since earlier that morning, was presumably doing her best to stay beside the object of her
dreams. Sure enough, Marion spotted her in the family
throng about the wheelchair, but she had no desire to
join Alma there. When the presentations were over
Carlo made a speech in the island dialect and was ap-
plauded long and loudly. The audience then made for
the food and drink, laughing and talking as they
streamed across the inner courtyards in their brilliant
array.

Luciana meanwhile was having a party of her own,
chattering to the local children in Sardinian, and all
afternoon Marion was free to walk about, to look and
listen and take her photographs. Soon spaces were
cleared and the villagers sat down to watch the dancing. Their round dances were not light and lively, but
grave performances, a more solemn version of the *sar-
dana* of northeastern Spain. She saw the castle maids
circling intently in one ring, then passed to another
where the onlookers were clapping in rhythm, as an
accordion played. There, leading off, were Carlo and
Alma.

Pliant and inviting, Alma advanced and retreated and advanced again. Her face shone, her full lips were parted; she looked only at him and the meaning of the look was unmistakable. As the music drew them together or sent her dancing away, every step was provocation, inducement or evasion, and her eyes were like bright emeralds.

Marion's first reaction was to think, *My God, what an exhibition!* How could anyone, she wondered, display her feelings to a man as nakedly as that? Her second, to acknowledge a weary weight of loneliness. What was she doing here? This festa, these people, with their noise and merrymaking, were utterly alien to her. She had blundered in among them rootless and lost, and she was trapped. And there was the other trap, too, infinitely worse and far more perilous, from which Georgette Lassalle in Paris was fighting to cut her free. Who could tell if they would win that case?

How far away it all was—her house at Saint-Cloud, her villa by the sea; all this past summer, the warmth, the lazy days, were far away and long ago and, for the time being at any rate, out of reach. It seemed impossible that she had ever had a husband. Stanni, a man to whom she was a pawn in a game and nothing else.

"What a sad face. Are you feeling homesick?"

She was sitting on a low wall and looked up to see Carlo before her. His voice brought her out of her dream and into the present, though he himself might have stepped out of the past, in that amazing costume.

All she could think of to say was, "Did Alma find another partner?"

"La mamma wanted her. She's back on duty for a while."

"What a remarkable person your grandmother is," sighed Marion, who had been admiring the old lady's stamina for hours. "She doesn't even begin to look tired;

you'd never think it was her eighty-seventh birthday.
And all your people seem to adore her."

"They respect her," Carlo replied with a serious
smile. "They love her too. She has always been here,
you see; one of the faithful few who never went off to
Rome or Milan when most of the great families left the
island. Peasants appreciate that; they're attached to
their land."

She could see what he meant. It was an attitude she
had to admit she agreed with.

"Why are you hiding away?" he wanted to know.
"I've been looking everywhere for you since this morning. I thought you must have fallen down a
mousehole."

"Oh, I've been taking pictures." She indicated the
camera slung over her shoulder. "I got some beauties,
too. I've never seen local color like this in my life before.
Everything's so real."

"It isn't local color," he retorted, with some heat. "All
that folklore business belongs down on the coast where
the visitors pay to see it; especially since the big developers got there, with their apartments and their great
palatial hotels. Have you heard of a man called Count
Marzotto? He's a rich Italian with a whole chain of
places in the tourist towns. Up here in the Barbagia,
we're against that sort of thing. We rather suspect our
fellow Sardinians who give in to cash and comfort; we
tend to despise them. We'll be hospitable, of course, and
make the foreigner welcome; but we don't want for-
eigners taking us over and we don't want the grind and
the treadmill of modern life."

"But modernization has its advantages, surely?"

"None at all," he said, flatly. "None that merits the
sacrifice of our own national character. Here in these
mountains, remember, we are the original inhabitants
of the island and proud of it. Since the very beginning,
whenever Sardinia was invaded, we took refuge here

in the mountains. Our direct ancestors lived in those
nuraghi before history was thought of. We are the old
blood, the hard core. We do without the telephone and
we have no television. And up in the highest villages,
we do without electricity, too."

Fiercely she rejoined, "Yes, that's all right for the
others, but what about you? You drive around in a
sports car, and you fly to the mainland when you want
to."

"I happen to need transport for my work and to help
our people here by creating a link with the rest of the
world."

"And to go off kidnapping children like an old-time
pirate!" The words were out before she could stop them
and though she clapped her hand to her mouth it was
too late. They hung in the air like a challenge, irretriev-
able. *Marion, Marion, what were you thinking of?*

They stared at one another, and his icy gaze cut
through her. His face might have been set in bronze, an
image dug from the earth of his own excavations. She
made as if to rise.

"Sit down!" he ordered furiously.

Pale and quaking, she obeyed and he sat on the coping beside her.

"Now, Mademoiselle," he said, with dreadful calm,
"you will please explain yourself."

"I have nothing to say."

"But you have said too much already."

She could not meet his eyes and turned away. Never,
never could she undo this ghastly mistake, nor accomplish her mission now. A fine detective she was! Georgette Lassalle didn't know what she was doing when
she relied on Marion.

"Look at me," he said. "At least have the courage to
tell me what was in your mind. I should not have
thought you were a person to evade an obligation."

"My thoughts are my own. I am under no obligation to tell you." But he had touched a sensitive spot.

"You have revealed your thoughts already. You passed an opinion on something that concerns me. I have a right to know what gave you the idea."

"No. I'd rather say no more about it." Her voice shook. "I used an unfortunate phrase. Do forgive me, it meant nothing." Then, with less hesitation, "I shall give my notice in at once."

"That would be a very convenient escape. I want an answer, please."

She would have given anything to be able to run from those accusing eyes, conscious as she was of the contemptible role she had agreed to play. She had come as a spy into his family, with intent to deceive, and what, after all, had any of it to do with her? She didn't know Paulette Arnaudy. Luciana was divinely happy where she was, loved and looked after. It was not for her to condemn these people. She had behaved abominably and the more she thought about it the worse she felt. Into the glacial pause drifted the noise of the festa. Carlo appeared to be waiting for her to come to a decision. And he was tenacious: he was going to stay there until she told him.

"Let's say I heard some gossip."

"You should not base an opinion upon gossip. You were referring to Luciana, of course."

"Luciana, yes," she nodded dejectedly.

Immediately, his tone changed. "I think you ought to know the facts," he said.

"I don't care about your facts!"

"In that case you shouldn't have raised the subject. But what you think happens to be important to me— important enough for me to give you an explanation."

"Oh, but you don't owe me an explanation!" she cried, in distress.

He ignored her. "I want you to know why, and from

what, we brought Luciana back into this family, where she belongs."

"Your family," she broke out. 'What does your family care for me? None of you need a foreigner coming here to tell you whether she approves or not."

He regarded her with an odd expression, in which anger seemed to be struggling with some other emotion; the desire to convince her, perhaps.

"If it were anyone but you, I wouldn't bother. You are a foreigner, but we have things in common, or so I have thought. I find an—an accord with you."

Marion recalled the Milanese girl's resentment at his supposed interest in her and replied, "This is what you should be saying to Alma, not me. She would understand you. Besides, she likes you."

"And you do not?"

"I didn't say that." As before, the words slipped out. "But you have, all of you, a sort of intolerance I simply can't accept. It puzzles me; if you must know, it revolts me. It might be more ... intelligible to Alma."

"We were discussing my niece, not Alma," he said shortly. "Keep to the point. Yes, I went to France to get her. I went on my mother's behalf; she had a perfect right to claim her granddaughter."

"By force? Illegally? A verdict had been given in favor of Luciana's mother, you know."

"An iniquitous verdict, quite unjustifiable. We would never recognize it, any more than we would recognize my brother's marriage with that—creature."

He spat the word with such venom that Marion almost jumped, but she made herself sit quite still. It was important to hear what he had to say.

She tried another approach. "You are devout, you Sardinians," she said, "you revere the sacraments. This marriage had the blessing of God—it was a sacrament."

"In this case the sacrament was a mockery. They were totally unsuited. My brother was under the influence of an adventuress. He didn't know what he was doing. It wasn't God, but the devil, who joined those two."

"That sounds blasphemous."

"You know nothing at all about it!" he exclaimed, exasperated. "One might as well listen to a blind man describing colors."

Marion turned and looked at him. "But what has she done, this woman, for you to speak of her like that? What has she done but love her husband?"

She thought he would choke. His dark face was suffused; when he spoke his voice was hard and metallic.

"Her husband? She stole her husband. Oh, yes, she stole him from the woman he chose and to whom he had pledged his word. I know that kind of thing hardly counts for you western Europeans. You don't think marriage itself important. For you it means as much or as little as you want it to, and then only so long as it isn't a nuisance."

She tried to interrupt but was silenced by an imperious wave of the hand. "With us, it is different. An oath is an oath. The given word is the given word and betrothal as binding as any marriage without that sacramental 'Yes' or the declaration in church. The breaking of a marriage promise brings shame on both families. It brings the vendetta."

"And that's a custom for savages. It doesn't belong to this day and age."

"It is our custom, and anyone who defies it does so at his peril. Oathbreaking carries terrible penalties. You fly to this woman's defense: do you know what she did?"

He looked beyond her, into the distance, his face strained and tense.

"It was a thunderclap out of a clear sky. Eficio and his fiancée were to be married. The guests were invited; everything was arranged. Then it was my brother's saint's day and they went to Cagliari for the pilgrimage and the festa. And unfortunately they also went to a nightclub later on, to see some new foreign cabaret.

"This Paulette Arnaudy was singing there. A beautiful voice, I believe; enchanting. She took one look at my brother and never left him alone all evening; she came to the table, singing her damned songs at him, pushing her face into his. And, he never said a word when they came home. He was distracted, lost in a dream.

"Next day and every day after that he went back to Cagliari until the group left the island. The singer was with them, and he followed her, the day before his wedding. He was bewitched. Angelina was busy with her preparations. She never suspected a thing; she was trying on her wedding dress when he boarded the boat. He was running away like a criminal, or a coward.

"Eficio left a short letter for my mother. It was dreadful. Our two families had always been friends; we were enemies overnight.

"My father didn't survive it long; his death was hastened by the shame and grief. I was in Rome, studying archeology, but of course I had to forget that—leave it all to take his place. I was head of the family from that day on."

His voice droned on in an empty monotone as though he were speaking of somebody else, but his expression betrayed despair and Marion was unaccountably moved. In a confused way she realized that she could not, should not, judge these people from her western standpoint. They were a separate breed with a different mentality, and their feelings, extravagant though they might seem, were worthy of respect.

"That must have been awful for you." She was careful not to sound sympathetic, fearing to offend him.

Carlo came back from the distance and looked at her again.

"I swore to revenge Angelina and to get my brother

away from that woman. He wanted his share of the
estate when my father died, and we had to sell farms
and cattle and land. He spent the lot with her—the
dolce vita in Milan. And when I went up there to talk
to him, I found he had married her. Given the creature
his name. There was nothing I could do, nothing!"

For a second he paused, then went on tonelessly,
"God punished him. Three years; then he died of cancer
in a matter of weeks. He had ruined his life and gone
through all his money. But he had fathered a child, and
she was a Terralba."

Once more his eyes quickened with anger. "And that
woman had the effrontery to ask us to contribute
toward her upbringing. When we offered to take Luciana, she refused. As though she could use Eficio's
daughter to make us repent and say we were sorry. We
took it to court and won, but then she went off to
France and applied to the courts there."

"Wasn't that a logical thing to do?"

"Logical for her, perhaps. Not for us. In short, the law,
French law, gave her custody and we could see the
child as and when she thought fit. She was free to do as
she thought fit with a Terralba! How do you imagine
we could accept any such immoral and ridiculous
ruling?"

Marion made no reply. There was none to make.

"What choice had we but to take justice into our own
hands—into my hands—and reclaim our own? That is
what I had to do, and I am proud to have done it."

He left her speechless. How in the world did one
make these passionate beings see reason? They
believed, heart and soul, in this justice of theirs, in their
morality and their right; and in that belief, grim and
oversimplified as it was, they acted with complete
sincerity.

"Well, tell me," he insisted, as though he had to force
something out of her, somehow make her approve,

"could we leave a Terralba with that sort of woman? In the false, vicious world she lives in? What would she have taught her? What kind of an example is she? You can't leave a child in an atmosphere like that."

"But do you even know Luciana's mother? You hate and detest her because you feel she's injured you. Is that a fair thing to do?"

His only response was a smile of contempt.

"A cabaret singer who picks up my brother as though he were something in a store window and carries him off in her pocket."

"There's no proof she didn't love him."

"How does a woman like that have any notion of what love is?" he demanded. "We do not wish to know her. She does not exist." He chopped the air, annihilating Paulette. "Nor do we wish to hear her spoken of."

"But she must be suffering so, without the child. Do you never think of that?"

"So much the better. It's all payment. She can pay forever and it still won't be enough. But you are being too kind; she hasn't the heart for suffering."

Marion finally attacked him, her voice shaking now with anger. "Who are you to decide that? I thought justice was supposed to be God's affair? And you call yourselves Christians. You go to mass every week of your lives and you never let anyone in this household miss it—it's a duty. But what about charity and tolerance, aren't they duties too? Because you happen to be rich, you act in this arbitrary fashion, as if the law didn't matter and you needn't bother with consequences. What sort of people are you?"

"We are fighting a depraved woman and protecting an innocent child from a thoroughly bad influence."

"How can you be so sure her influence is bad? You condemn her without a hearing, you make no attempt to discover facts. You don't know her. You can't have the remotest idea of whether she's what you think she is or not."

"Didn't you hear what I told you?" He was as incensed as she. "She ruined my brother, caused a scandal, and she set two decent families at loggerheads."

"And what about your brother, had he nothing to do with it? He was a grown man, not a small boy; he was responsible for his own actions. If he married her, he must have thought she was worth marrying. And from what I know of you, I can't see any Terralba giving his name to a common trollop."

"She put a spell on him. He was out of his mind."

"Oh, spells! We're not in the Middle Ages."

"You talk like an ignorant schoolgirl." For some reason, his pitying gaze was deeply wounding. "But you're old enough to know what base instincts mean. My brother pursued that woman like a dog going after a bitch. He was led by every base instinct he had."

She protested violently. "How do you know? How can you see into anybody's motives? There's a secret side to everyone and you can be as close as you like, but no one sees it, ever. You can't paint this woman black enough, but you've never even met her. It's all presumption, supposition. You've never as much as said 'good morning' to her, or let her speak a word on her own behalf. You said just now she hasn't any heart; well, that's a frightful thing to say. What do you understand about her heart? She was a cabaret singer. What's wrong with that? Nobody has anything against cabaret singers these days; it's a profession, like any other profession, and some very nice people go in for it. You can't sit there like judge and jury and hand out pains and penalties, because she sang in a nightclub."

Carlo screwed his eyes up and looked at her attentively. "You make a remarkably strong speech for the defense," he said.

Marion blushed and turned away. "I hate injustice,"

she replied, in a neutral tone. "And if there were faults, surely your brother paid for them, dying so young? You can hardly want to take revenge on the dead?"

"But it is my brother whom I wish to avenge. If he had never met that woman, he would still be here. And poor Angelina too; instead she is in a convent."

"But that woman, as you call her, didn't necessarily intend those things. They just happened that way, that's all. She's not to blame just because you take everything to extremes and see a broken engagement as some sort of unpardonable crime."

"We are what we are," he said in a stony voice. "We abide by our principles, and that is one of them; part of life as we see it, of our customs and our traditions. It is not our fashion to tolerate desertion and betrayal. Others may do so, but we will not compromise, and because of that, though we are isolated, we survive." He stopped and shook his head. "You cannot be expected to see it. You belong to the west and we do not."

To this she had no answer. Indignation, ardor and fury had evaporated, leaving her more detached than ever, inexplicably an intruder into this purely family problem. Suddenly she was aware of the festivities again, whose noise had gone unheard during that tight-rope conversation, and she gave a deep sigh.

"What is it?" he demanded instantly.

She said to herself, *No, it's quite true, I can't see it at all.* Then aloud, "I do apologize for interfering when it's nothing to do with me. Forgive me."

His manner softened and he touched her shoulder. "Let's stop fighting and forget it. You're supposed to be happy on a day like this."

She wanted to pull away from him, but still the strange weariness possessed her and she did not move.

"Come on, Marion, smile. Just try."

For the first time he was calling her by her name. Hesitantly, she smiled.

"That's better. If you knew how much better, you'd smile more often."

Such powers of persuasion were too strong for her and she went with him, unprotesting. Gently but firmly he propelled her through the crowd to the buffet and put a glass in her hand.

"There you are, French champagne. Your health, Mademoiselle."

The outburst of a few moments ago was as though it had never been. He watched her as she drank and gave her a second glass. The wine was cool and golden and bubbling, and it washed the tension away. She could see he was no longer in the least ferocious, and his eyes were warm and friendly.

"Happier now?"

"Much happier," she said and meant it. All at once she longed to take part in everything and to enjoy herself.

"Come and dance."

He relieved her of her camera and gave it to a maid behind the table, then steered her to the dancing, disregarding her half-hearted protests.

"But I don't know how!"

"It's easy, you'll soon learn. Just follow me."

They plunged into the circle. As the little Sardinian band beat out the rhythm, Carlo's fingers curled round hers and he indicated the steps, clicking his tongue against his teeth with a kissing sound. Suddenly elated without knowing why, she gave herself up to the dance. It was so long since she had felt like this. Everyone sang and the pace quickened. Her hair fell loose and Carlo, laughing, singing, reached over and helped her push it back, looking into eyes as joyous, shining, youthful as his own. With a kind of astonishment he leaned down and his lips brushed her cheek, so lightly he hardly seemed to touch her.

"Oh." Still laughing, she tilted her head away and

found Alma behind her, mouth set, the picture of outrage.

Scarlet with embarrassment, suddenly feeling guilty and almost physically sick with shame, she stammered an excuse in Carlo's direction, broke from the singing, dancing circle, turned and fled.

BACK IN DOWNTOWN PARIS Monsieur Perdrière picked up the telephone receiver, which was buzzing to indicate an intercom call. He listened for a second, then said, "Send him right in."

Lassalle, sitting at his left side, said simply, "Maresco?"

Perdrière nodded. "He's right on time. He's probably been on pins and needles waiting for this confrontation for days."

Remembering the tall, lean man who had left her office in such a rage two weeks earlier Lassalle nodded gravely. Somehow, the prey always knows when the hunters are closing in on it; and in the case of Stanislas Maresco, closing in had been a ridiculously easy thing to do. The man didn't arouse any sympathy in Georgette Lassalle, who was trained to seek out vulnerabilities.

Marion, for instance, had been a huge, quivering ball of vulnerability the first time they had met; Paulette Arnaudy was becoming that way, despite her enormous acting ability; but Maresco . . . always cold, always on his guard. . . . Maresco had set himself up as Lassalle's adversary even before they had met, and by coming to her with a closed mind, he had actually prevented her from feeling any sympathy for him at all.

Typically, as he came in the door to Perdrière's office, Maresco nodded perfunctorily at her, then at Perdrière. As he found a seat in the corner of the room opposite the two lawyers, another man, a short, balding man in a rumpled blue suit, hurried breathlessly through the double wooden doors and bowed, gasping for breath, to his two colleagues.

"My attorney," said Maresco drily from his corner. "Monsieur André."

As Maresco inspected his nails impatiently, André shook hands with Perdrière and Lassalle, then opened the slim Samsonite briefcase he held and extracted an equally slender file folder.

"A deposition," he explained, handing it to Perdrière, "from Carole Jordan, the sister of my client, attesting to his character and to his competence in the running of Maraval Perfumes, which, of course, no longer exists as a firm."

"Thanks to Marion," Maresco observed sarcastically.

"My client finds it difficult to understand," the little man went on, in a slightly louder voice, "why his wife would wish to dispose of a profitable business he was making even more profitable by his labors on her behalf."

Lassalle and Perdrière exchanged a significant look. Maresco had evidently not told his attorney the whole truth.

"Perhaps you would care to peruse the material in this file folder, Monsieur," offered Perdrière, handing it across the desk toward him. "You are, naturally, aware that there are several issues involved here, civil as well as criminal."

"Of course," André confirmed, hefting the file folder with his right hand. "My client is not contesting the divorce action. He is just as surprised as anyone to discover that his first wife, whom he presumed dead, is in reality alive. The legal tangle results from an unfortunate misunderstanding. . . ."

As the little man went smoothly on, Georgette Lassalle had to bite her tongue to keep from interrupting him. So that was the tack Maresco intended to take—pretend ignorance, shrug his shoulders and concede issues where he hadn't any choice in the face of the masses of evidence against him!

In a courtroom, that tactic would have stood him in good stead; and if this case were allowed to get to court, then that weasel Maresco might just squeeze out of some of his just desserts. Doing a quick mental tabulation of the contents of the file folder, Lassalle began to feel more confident. In terms of hard evidence, of depositions, of witnesses, of financial statements, they had enough to convict him on serious criminal charges.

Perdrière had interrupted the flow of words from Monsieur André and was indicating the file folder again. "Before the conference, I really feel you ought to look at the material evidence against your client," he insisted in a gentle voice. "Perhaps you would care to use the adjoining study . . . ?"

André bowed, and with a frown at Maresco, who merely shrugged, turned and entered Perdrière's study with the bulging file folder. For the next ten minutes, Lassalle and Maresco conducted a little war of nerves by glaring at one another from opposite corners of the room, until Perdrière was about to suggest that Maresco go get himself a cup of coffee at the receptionist's post outside the door.

Suddenly, the door to the study flew open and a discomposed M. André emerged, wiping his brow nervously, his coat draped over his arm and his tie loosened at his throat. Dropping the file folder on Perdrière's desk, he bowed again and gasped, "I shall need time to prepare my client's answers to your material."

Smiling triumphantly, Perdrière suggested, "Shall we reconvene one week from today, then?"

"That would be perfect," said André, and shooting a dirty look at his client, the little man rushed from Perdrière's office. Frowning uncertainly, Maresco rose and followed him.

Carole had assured him that nobody had found that
report, and yet these two had somehow got their hands
on it. And now . . . what had they gathered that his
web of half-truths and protestations could not turn
away? Maresco felt his stomach sink as he remembered
the look that had passed between the two lawyers.

It sank again as he picked up the receiver of his telephone in la Celle Saint-Cloud and heard Lassalle's
voice on the other end of the line.

"I think we ought to talk, Monsieur Maresco," she
said. "You may call your attorney in if you wish."

"I haven't got one," he spat bitterly. "André's taken
himself off the case."

"That does simplify things," she remarked. "Just the
two of us, then. Where shall we meet, your home or my
office?"

Maresco shrugged, a useless gesture when talking on
the phone, then said, "My home. That office of yours is
like a museum."

"Very well, then. Expect me in twenty minutes."

After hanging up, Maresco felt suddenly weak. His
whole world seemed to be crumbling around him, and
there wasn't a thing he could do about it. His thrashing
about had done him more harm than good, as he had
alienated every form of authority that could help him
out of this predicament.

His sister had an attorney and was insisting on being
tried separately from her brother. His own lawyer had
told him he would not defend him, since in light of
what he had read in Perdrière's study, Maresco was
indefensible. He felt like an animal caught by one leg in
a trap, reduced to gnawing off the captured limb in
order to survive, taking the risk of bleeding to death in
the process. And now Lassalle wanted to see him—for
what? Hadn't she taken her pound of flesh in Perdrière's office?

Twenty minutes later, wearing a pale blue suit and

matching boots, Georgette Lassalle rang the doorbell of
the Maresco residence in Saint-Cloud; the man who
opened it did so cavalierly, with a drink in one hand
and his pipe in the other, and judging by his breath, the
drink in his hand was not the first he had had today.
Steeling herself for an unpleasant scene, Lassalle entered the living room after shutting the front door
behind her. She sat down slowly on an overstuffed
armchair, finally locating her "host" by the sound of
ice cubes being stirred in a drink of some kind. As he
swung himself around the doorway leading from the
kitchen, she said brightly, "Are you ready to discuss
your position in this case, Monsieur?"

"Sure," he replied, gesturing expansively. "Go ahead
and kick a man when he's down."

"That wasn't what I had in mind," she reproved
him. "I've come to advise you."

"What?" he hooted. "I don't believe that!"

"You didn't believe that Marion was alive, either,
and yet she is."

"All right, all right," he growled, settling at last into
a chair opposite hers. "What *is* my position in this
case?"

"You may not be contesting the divorce action, but
the suit being brought against you is no longer a civil
one. It is not necessary to prove grounds for divorce if
one of the marriage partners is a bigamist. Bigamy is a
criminal charge."

Maresco gulped hard as the color drained from his
cheeks. His reaction pleased Lassalle, since a frightened
man would be more pliable than a defiant, rebellious
one.

"Dora?" he managed to gasp.

Lassalle nodded grimly. "Duplicating the research of
the firm hired by Félicien Maraval, I spoke to Dora on
the telephone. She escaped from behind the Iron Curtain not long ago. She's living in Belgium; and she has

agreed to testify at your trial." Lassalle paused to let the effect of these words sink in. Maresco looked ill.

"In addition to the charge of bigamy, there are of course the charges of conspiracy, which your sister shares with you, and of fraud. We have hard evidence that you have been stealing patents and diverting funds from Maraval Perfumes in order to set up a company of your own."

"I was doing it as a surprise for Marion!" he blurted out, his eyes wide with fear. "Really! Maraval Perfumes was so large and unwieldy—this smaller company would have been far more economical and easier to run—Marion could have run it herself!"

Lassalle shot him a scornful look. "Do you really expect me, or a judge, to swallow that nonsense? It may have fooled Monsieur André temporarily, but it simply doesn't stand up to the depositions and financial statements in our case file on you."

Maresco seemed to shrink physically at that point. His trump lie had been rejected. There was no longer any hope of extricating himself from this mess.

"If the case comes to court."

Maresco looked up, startled. "If?" he demanded.

Lassalle nodded. "It needn't ever reach the courts," she confirmed.

He snorted with derision, not sure whether to laugh or cry.

"Bigamy, conspiracy and fraud, and it needn't ever get to court!" he scoffed. "That would take a miracle!"

"In a way, you bought yourself a miracle when you married a woman who valued her privacy. It's far better than you deserve, but Marion would prefer to settle this as quietly as possible, without the publicity and scandal that a court case would bring."

"In other words, if I cooperate with all her wishes . . . ?"

"Oh, you don't get off that easily. You must leave in

her possession a signed confession of all your criminal misdeeds, as a guarantee that once out of her life, you will never reenter it. You must also agree to leave France, forever, since the charges will still be on the books, and should you return, you would be liable to criminal prosecution."

"And the signed confession in Marion's possession. . . . "

"Would put you away for twenty years," stated Lassalle serenely. "Would you like some time to think about it?"

Maresco shook his head wearily. "No, that isn't necessary."

"Good. Meet me in Perdrière's office tomorrow and we can get everything out of the way very quickly."

"What about my sister?"

"Monsieur Perdrière is contacting the magistrate now. You can call her and tell her to pack her bags— and to meet us at Perdrière's office tomorrow, about ten o'clock."

Ashen, Maresco nodded mindlessly as Lassalle rose with a smile on her face.

"Don't bother seeing me out," she said, heading for the front door.

Paulette Arnaudy was seated in the visitor's chair opposite the tidy oak desk when the lawyer arrived back at her office.

The singer had been crying since coming to see Georgette Lassalle, for the tear streaks were still visible on her cheeks, and a seasoned and popular entertainer never left the house without a perfect face. Clutching a dainty lace-edged handkerchief, Arnaudy turned mournful dark eyes toward Lassalle as she came in the door.

"You're late," she murmured brokenly.

"It was unavoidable," explained the detective. "I'm sorry you had to be kept waiting."

Lassalle's client smiled bravely. "If it was for good news, then I don't mind waiting," she said, dabbing at her eyes with the crumpled handkerchief.

Briskly, Lassalle removed a file from the cabinet behind her desk and opened it in front of her. As Arnaudy scanned the first page of the latest report from Marion, the lawyer removed her overcoat and draped it over a wooden stand hidden behind the door.

"That is the latest news," she told the singer, swiveling the folder around so that Paulette Arnaudy had to continue reading upside down for a moment. With a sniff, she straightened in her seat and readjusted the coat around her shoulders.

"My agent has given me a rather complete description of the castle and its surroundings, and I agree with her assessment that the countryside would be unsuitable for our attempt. We would have far better success in the town of Núoro."

"Whatever you say," affirmed the singer, beginning to brighten.

Lassalle looked up, frowning. "I have a plan," she began, "that has fairly good chances of success, if the timing is right. That's a big *if*. One slip could scuttle it."

"Madame, I am desperate," said Arnaudy brokenly. "I would travel any distance, take any foolish risks, if I felt that in the end I would have my little girl back again."

"I'm glad you feel that way," said Lassalle, "because I was about to ask you whether you could free yourself to fly down to Sardinia with me to liberate the child."

Paulette Arnaudy cocked her head and raised an eyebrow in puzzlement. "Liberate?" she wondered aloud. "That sounds almost as if—"

"It is exactly what it sounds like," declared the detective. "My plan is to go to Sardinia and kidnap Lucy away from the Terralbas. The move is illegal only as long as we are on Sardinian soil; once back in France, we would be protected by the ruling of the courts that gave you custody of the child to begin with. Our only risk would be in leaving the island with Lucy."

The singer pondered the ramifications of this for a moment, then asked slowly, "What about your agent down there? Couldn't she—"

Lassalle shook her head emphatically. 'She is another client of mine, doing me a favor. I promised her that she would not be asked to do anything illegal, even temporarily illegal."

"I'll go," stated the singer firmly. "When are we leaving?"

"I am expecting one more report from my agent, containing the timetables of the various family members for the next little while. With that in our hands, we can make final plans. Does that suit you?"

Smiling hopefully, Paulette Arnaudy said, "Just so long as Lucy can spend Christmas here with her mother, where she belongs. Thank you, for all you've done."

Her coat slung over her shoulders, Paulette Arnaudy left, still dabbing at her eyes. Lassalle, seated at her desk, turned the pages of Marion's last report until she came to the part that was disturbing. She read it through once again, then closed the folder, folded her arms over it and rested her chin on her folded arms, her forehead furrowed in thought.

Marion's letters, at first so informative and objective, had begun to show signs of great reluctance to participate further in this project. The influence of the Terralba family was having a disturbing effect on her, eroding away her resolve, creating doubts in her mind of the wisdom of taking the child away. Perhaps it had been a mistake to send someone in Marion's state of mind on such a delicate mission—Florence would have

been perfect in this task. Florence had always had a
will of iron and the ability to divorce herself com
pletely from sentimentality. . . .

Ah, well! What was done was done. Marion had in
gratiated herself into the Terralba clan, had earned
their trust, had weaseled enough information out o
everyone to give Lassalle's plan the edge it needed t
make it feasible. However, what was needed to make i
successful, beyond a shadow of a doubt, was the coop
eration of Lucy's governess at the end, and judging b
the tone of Marion's last few letters, they might not b
able to count on Marion's help in a pinch. . . .

Wondering irrelevantly whether Marion was a hap
pier person than had been put on the plane some week
ago, Georgette opened the report file again and rerea
the paragraph in which Marion's doubts had been ex
pressed. They were sincere and well expressed, causin
Lassalle to feel that no amount of coaxing and cajolin
would change Marion's mind.

Her eyes caught on one sentence, which had been th
recurring theme lately: "Luciana is surrounded by lov
and affection, in surroundings which are familiar t
her—I really believe that the best thing for her woul
be a compromise worked out between Arnaudy an
the Terralbas."

Well, perhaps Marion was right. The detective con
sidered for a moment the hectic schedule of an enter
tainer, the parade of nannies and governesses tha
seemed to punctuate the lives of most film stars' chil
dren, the newspaper articles that kept popping up wit
disturbing regularity concerning the child of this o
that actor or singer who had been arrested, or taken a
overdose of drugs.

Impatiently, Georgette shook herself free of this rev
erie. Paulette Arnaudy was her client—had kept her o
a retainer for the three years since Lucy was kidnap
ped. And her client wanted Lucy back. Her duty wa

simple; she would do what she was paid to do. Marion could luxuriate in sentiments of trust and sympathy, all those miles away in Sardinia. Lassalle could not afford them right now. If Paulette Arnaudy wanted to negotiate with the Terralbas—and she might, if Marion's next letter took the next logical step and she asked to be taken off the assignment—then all well and good. But Lassalle would not attempt to force a compromise on her client.

CHAPTER 12

Carlo departed for Rome a few days after the festa and she did not see him after the dance. Before leaving, he visited the nursery but only Francesca was there with his niece. How was Mademoiselle? Mademoiselle begged to be excused this morning; she had a migraine.

In fact, Marion was trying to sort herself out and, as a result, mailed a letter to Lassalle that same day, giving up her assignment. She had been under a strain, she said, when she took it on, had not really known what it was all about and now realized that she was quite un-suited to the work. Could a replacement be sent as quickly as possible?

She could endure the position no longer. Given the choice, Marion would have tendered her notice and left without delay, but since that would have been neither sensible nor fair she merely asked Georgette Lassalle to relieve her as soon as she could. She wanted very much to pack up and go before Carlo came back.

She returned to her duties, however, despite her private turmoil, and the life of the castle went on. Conscientiously she saw to Luciana's lessons, while at the same time doing her best to keep out of the family's way. But this was not altogether easy, for something like genuine friendship had sprung up between them during the last few weeks. She had fallen into the habit of playing cards or dominoes with Maria Pia in the drawing room after dinner, and would chat for hours to Donna Eleonora, who was making great efforts with her French. With Alma, of course, everything was already changed; the girl's open hostility, though all too understandable, added to Marion's wretchedness.

Only with Luciana could she be normal and happy. Indeed she grew steadily more attached to this winning, charming child and more and more distressed to think of the battle over her, with each side convinced of its own right and each, apparently, motivated by pure love. Luciana was not yet of an age to suffer from the impossible situation, but the results might be more serious. Now she was bubbling with high spirits, but how would that sunny nature be affected as the tug-of-war developed? Marion wished devoutly that she had never known her, never known any of them.

Why, oh why, was she so involved with them all? Why this inner anguish at the thought of leaving so soon? Perhaps because she had nobody to go back to? Nothing awaited her in France but the troubles and worries she had escaped from.

Not many weeks after her arrival she had had a report from Georgette Lassalle on the case in progress against Stanni Maresco and had replied by return mail:

Don't send me any more news until the hearing is over. I don't even want to think about him. He'll overshadow the rest of my life as it is, but I mean to try and forget, as far as I can, how blind and stupid I have been. I still feel so bitterly humiliated, and the thought of anything in any way connected with the subject makes it worse. I want to put it out of my

mind while I'm here and try to get some peace, if I
can.

Lassalle entirely agreed and for weeks sent only the
letters from M. Perdrière, routed through Lassalle's
office. These he kept as short as possible and confined to
essentials—business details concerning the sale of Maraval Perfumes. Out of respect for her privacy, he refrained from mentioning his difficulties with her husband who, between the legal proceedings and his
complete inability to discover Marion's whereabouts,
was caught in an impasse and struggling like a mad-
man to escape.

STANDING CONCEALED AT A WINDOW, Alma watched
Luciana and her governess drive off in the dogcart with
Giuseppe, accompanied by Maria Pia and the duenna,
their ample skirts spread around them on the seat. She
waited until they were safely through the main gate
and the sound of hoofs had died away, before darting to
Marion's room. It was unlikely that anyone would be
about, but she carried a French book, borrowed previously in case a maid appeared.

Marion's behavior had been very suspicious for some
time. She was obviously expecting a very important
letter. Why else would she collect her mail directly
from the postman every day? And since discovering
the lie regarding Marion's feelings for Carlo, Alma had
decided that everything Marion did was suspect.

So, appointing herself detective for the household,
Alma was about to embark on a search of Marion's
room. It was also a convenient excuse to look for evidence that there was something between Marion and
Carlo. Alma was wildly jealous, and she had to know
the truth. The Frenchwoman's disavowals when told
of Alma's grand passion had at first allayed suspicion,
but since then, Marion's behavior with Carlo had done
nothing to inspire confidence. Doubt and alarm filled

Alma's soul, and she was not above a little burglary in quest of reassurance.

But Marion's room could not have been more innocent: a tidy, feminine room, with everything neatly in place. A leather blotter on the rosewood desk contained only envelopes, writing paper and some postcards bought in Nûoro. So where did she keep the letters the postman brought?

Alma opened a drawer, but it held nothing of any interest. Another kept stamps and cigarettes, several rolls of film and an address book, which she leafed through. Nothing there either, and she recognized none of the names.

Footsteps from the tiled passage outside sent her racing to the shelves in an obvious show of returning the book. But the maid passed the door and Alma hurried to finish her search.

The desk itself was locked. Not daring to force it open, she was about to give up, with regret, and leave quietly when a ray of sunlight caught something under the glass-domed clock. Only Alma's keen eye would have observed it. Lifting the dome, she slid her hand beneath the clock and found a small brass key; it fit the desk perfectly.

There were letters in the pigeon holes, but they were all in French and could not be from Carlo. Much discouraged, she was on the point of closing the lid when she saw the edge of a piece of paper protruding from a crack. She put her fingernail in the groove and a secret drawer slid open in the body of the desk itself.

The sheet of paper she had found was covered in scribbled notes in what she recognized as Marion's handwriting. She was about to replace it when Carlo's name leaped out at her. She did not read French readily, but a line or two was enough. She went over it more than once before, incredulous and fuming, she grasped what it meant.

She clawed feverishly at the inside of the drawer,
but there was nothing else there, so she folded the paper with great care and thrust it down the front of her
dress. Then she relocked the desk and put the key back
in its place; and when she left the room Alma looked
much happier than she had upon entering it.

Marion might have noticed the theft had she been
less miserable and preoccupied. But as it was, she was
anxiously awaiting the news from Georgette Lassalle
that would set her free and give her a pretext for leaving; while every day, though she dreaded the thought
of departure, she grew more frantic in case Carlo returned before she had gone.

The long-awaited letter arrived at last. Georgette
was pained to learn of her decision; she could not, of
course, force her to stay, but it would not be easy to get
Luciana out of a place like Castel Terralba, and did
Marion realize that if she gave up now, when all the
plans were laid, they might have to use other means?
Things could become extremely complicated, if not
dangerous.

"We were intending to act in the very near future,"
wrote Mlle Lassalle, "and I think we have covered all
eventualities. Could I ask you to postpone your move
and remain there to help us? It won't be for long."

"Impossible," Marion replied by telegram, "am giving notice for end of month."

It was now the twentieth of December and Christmas was upon them. She informed the Marchesa that
domestic problems called her back to France, and she
would have to leave. Donna Eleonora was both surprised and sorry. Could she not persuade her to stay?
But Marion stood firm.

"I can't tell you how sad it is to lose you, especially
now that Luciana knows you, and she's so fond of you.
We shall have to find somebody else, I'm afraid, and
these changes are not good for her."

She seemed genuinely upset, which made Marion feel more ashamed than ever. It was certainly high time to go. She was already much too drawn to this family she had come to betray, like a thief in the night. But there was absolutely no reason to betray them, and she would not do it.

When the mistress of Castel Terralba announced the news that evening, everyone looked horrified. Must Marion really go? And why so soon? Their French guest had obviously earned a place in their affections. Alma alone seemed pleased, in a spiteful way, but Marion ignored her somewhat peculiar glance. She had more than Alma to worry about, and the girl's attitude had put an end to any question of friendship between them. She could not suspect the weapon the other possessed to use against her.

IN THE MORNING mail, another letter arrived, one that could shape her whole future. She sat down to steady herself. Then with trembling fingers, she hurried back to study it in the privacy of her room.

Georgette Lassalle had kept silence for several months on the subject of her investigations, as requested, but the confidential report she now submitted was so astounding, so unequivocal and so pregnant with consequence that her client was almost too shaken to believe it. The relief contained in that thick envelope seemed too good to be true.

Was this at last the end of the long tunnel into which she had strayed, too young and simple to see where she was going and where she had wandered, baffled and bruised, in the dark? Misery had become almost second nature to her, and now this document, with its clipped, police-court phrases, came as a message of liberation.

Although her life and work in Sardinia had partly dulled the wretchedness, the smallest remembrance served to bring it back to haunt her, and she had re-

signed herself to spending the rest of her days a pris-
oner in that tunnel. Her admirable Lady Detective,
however, had ferreted out the agency employed by Félicien Maraval to check up on his future son-in-law.
Their discovery was incredible. Dazed at first, then
with increasing eagerness, Marion read and reread the
letter.

"No wonder," it ran, "your father was so upset at the
thought of your contemplated marriage. Stanislas
Maresco had no legal right to contract any union, civil
or religious, for the good and sufficient reason that he
had married a woman named Dora Bekowa in Yugo-
slavia ten years previously. This present marriage is
therefore invalid."

So that was Dora. The few syllables of her name
were like a passport out of prison, an order of release.

From this starting point, it appeared, Georgette Lassalle had discovered all about Dora. She had been a
convinced militant, much concerned with politics, and
when she married the student Stanislas her political
activities continued as before. This, it seemed, had led
to differences, since she had been far more deeply
"committed" than he. Then, in the course of a skirmish
in which several of her fellow campaigners had been
killed and others arrested, she had vanished. Her young
husband had managed to escape to safety.

When he had been informed by his attorney of what,
on Marion's behalf, Lassalle had found out, he claimed
to have acted in good faith, believing that Dora had
paid the price of her revolutionary activities and left
him free; ten years had passed, his country was on the
other side of the Iron Curtain. That chapter of his life
was over. His lawyer had quit in disgust, but the Lady
Detective had convinced Maresco of his error. Either
from negligence, or from motives which she refrained
from enlarging upon, he had laid himself open to a
charge of bigamy.

This made progress easier. Once Stanni recognized his true position, and that the wisest thing he could do was to keep quiet, he cooperated. He cooperated in the dissolution of his marriage to the Māraval heiress; and too terrified to do anything but sign every paper the lawyer laid before him when the business was sold, he cooperated with Perdrière.

The nightmare was finished, but it had left its mark on Marion. From now on, her instinctive reaction to any man would be one of distrust. She had lost her illusions and bitterness had taken their place; and though the tragedy was behind her, she knew that something of her youth was lost forever.

MEANWHILE PAULETTE ARNAUDY was sweeping through the door to Georgette Lassalle's Paris office. "I came as soon as you called," she sang out. "Have you received the final report? Is everything ready to go? When are we leaving for Sardinia? I've bought a tree already, and Lucy can help me decorate it. It's going to be such a wonderful Christmas"

"There's been a snag." These words cut through Arnaudy's monologue like a sharp knife. Like a damaged inflated toy, she folded slowly sideways and fell into the chair in front of Lassalle's desk, a dismayed look on her face.

"What . . . what did you say?" She inquired faintly. "A snag?"

Wearily, Georgette Lassalle looked up and nodded. She rustled the paper in her hand and said, "My agent is resigning from the case. Our plan will have to be postponed until I have managed to replace her."

"Must it?" asked the singer, tears starting in her eyes. "Can't we go ahead without her?"

"Our chances of success would be so slim that I simply couldn't risk it," the lawyer told her. "I was counting on her to keep the family unaware of the child's disappearance until we could get out of their reach. But now. . . ." With a shrug, Lassalle leaned back in her chair.

"But you promised me," Arnaudy squeaked in a little-girl voice. "You promised me she would be home for Christmas! I've already made such plans!" Tears welled up in those famous dark eyes and spilled over, streaming down her cheeks like raindrops on a windowpane.

"I cannot sanction the operation under these circumstances," said Georgette, gently, but standing firm. "The risks would simply be too great."

"Not for me!" declaimed Paulette Arnaudy. "I'll go there alone, then. Give me the information from your agent."

The detective placed the letter from Marion on top of the folder and put it back in the filing cabinet.

"For your own sake, I refuse. You are upset. Perhaps later, when you are thinking more clearly—"

"I've never thought more clearly in my life!" exclaimed Paulette. "And I'm sure that all the money I've paid you over the past three years is more than enough to buy a look at your agent's precious report." Her eyes glittered, but not from tears. Georgette Lassalle was looking at the face of a truly desperate woman, one who would fly by herself to Sardinia and carry off the child who had been forcefully taken from her three years ago. Sighing, she reopened the filing cabinet and removed the folder from the drawer. Finally she looked up from her slightly bent-over position and said, "All right, then, we'll both go. But I want you to know from the start that I don't hold out any great hopes for our success."

Seeming a little reassured by these words, the singer settled back slightly in her seat. "And Lucy will be home for Christmas?"

"Either Lucy will spend Christmas here, or we'll

both spend it in a Sardinian prison," sighed Lassalle.
"Fortunately, the Sardinian authorities view passion as
a form of insanity; so, if we're caught, and you can
display the same level of feeling that you showed me
just now, we shouldn't fare too badly."

"We won't be caught," declared the singer
haughtily. "You are much too clever for that, Mademoiselle Lassalle."

With that, she was out the door, humming a snatch
of her latest recording. Lassalle did some quick mental
rearranging. Yes, it was possible that they could take
the child and squeeze past the police cordons. But one
thought kept coming back to torment her: a compromise really would be best for the child. How was it that
Marion seemed to be the only one thinking of the child?
The Terralbas had snatched Lucy away to salvage
their pride, and Paulette was determined to have her
back because of the rights that the court had given
her—had waited three years for the opportunity to retrieve what was legally hers, without thought for the
child's memories of her, which must be dim, if they had
survived at all.

Taking pen in hand, Georgette began to work out the
timing of her revised plan. Among the items in the
folder was a recent airlines schedule of flights to Sardinia, which she placed on her desk next to Marion's
handwritten family timetable. Lassalle had mailed her
a first draft of the original plan—should Marion be told
that a version of that plan was soon to be initiated?
No—Marion had developed scruples; she might warn
the Terralbas. And the detective's loyalties, as had been
so crassly pointed out to her by Paulette Arnaudy, had
already been purchased, over three years, on the instal-
ment plan.

At last, it was done. Lassalle surveyed the completed
schedule, going over it again in her mind, visualizing

the two of them actually boarding the plane and dis-
embarking again, hiring a car and driving into town.

Slowly, she nodded her head, trying to force herself
to feel some enthusiasm and anticipation. The plan was
risky, just the way she liked them; on the margins of
the law, also the way she liked them; and not in the
best interests of anyone concerned—Paulette, Lucy,
Marion, the Terralbas. The innocent would suffer along
with the guilty. Her attorney's conscience rebelled at
that, and was brutally repressed by the cold, hard facts
of the case. Lassalle had accepted money to accomplish
a task; that task would be completed.

Sighing heavily, she folded the paper containing the
plan, scribbled some instructions to her receptionist on
another sheet of paper, to be left on his desk and acted
upon when he had returned from lunch, and put her
coat on. She wasn't really hungry, but the actions of
driving her car to a restaurant, ordering a meal and
chewing it would give her something to do until it was
time to put Plan B, Arnaudy Case into operation.

CHAPTER 13

The white Alfa Romeo drew up in the courtyard and its owner emerged to open the garage and put away the car. It was nine o'clock in the morning and he had driven all night, but since he was more hungry than tired he immediately visited the kitchen to demand an enormous breakfast.

After eating he went upstairs and knocked at the door of his mother's room. The Marchesa, just getting up, was delighted to see him.

"Carlo. We never expected you. You should have let me know. When did you get here?"

"I came on the night plane and I didn't fancy staying in Olbia. The car was there, so I came straight home."

"But you must be exhausted."

"Not too bad. I can rest this afternoon. How is la mamma?"

"Very well. She—"

"And Luciana?"

"Very well, too. She and Francesca are going with

Giuseppe to the village. It's market day, and Christmas time, you know."

He frowned. "Francesca? Why not Mademoiselle?"

"No. About Mademoiselle—"

"I'll just go and catch Luciana," and he was off. His mother sighed and left her news for another time.

He saw the trap in the courtyard as he crossed the hall, Luciana and the maid already in the back seat. Beside them stood Marion, giving final instructions and advice. In two rapid strides he joined them.

"Good morning, Luciana." The little girl threw herself into his arms. "I brought you a lovely doll from Rome."

He hugged her and looked over her head at Marion, who rather wished the ground would open and swallow her up.

"Good morning." He spoke as though this were something serious and important.

Her "Good morning" came with a small gasp and she had gone pale.

"You're thinner," he said.

"Thinner? Oh, I don't think so—"

He set the child down in the cart again.

"Happy shopping, pet. Bring some candy for me. Coachman, drive on."

"When can I see my doll, Uncle Carlo?" enquired Luciana, anxiously.

"As soon as you come back; she won't fly away. Off you go, now, or you'll be too late and there won't be anything left."

Giuseppe made an encouraging noise at the horse and the trap moved forward, leaving Marion and Carlo alone.

"Didn't you want to see the market?" he asked with a smile. "I thought you loved these typical occasions."

"I've a lot to do." If only she had finished her packing before he came home, out of the blue, like this. He kept his eyes on her, smiling, and the steady regard disturbed her. For the sake of saying something, she asked, "Did you have a good journey?"

"Splendid."

With an effort she stood still, outwardly calm.

"I wanted to get here quickly."

"Oh."

"I missed you very much."

She felt the blood well into her cheeks and turned as though to go indoors.

"Marion."

"Yes?" Again the sound of her name on his lips made her happy.

"I have been thinking about what you said."

"What I said?"

"The night before I left. Luciana's mother—you remember?"

"Oh, that. Yes."

"And," he declared, "I wish to be neither unjust, nor barbaric, nor a savage."

But I—"

"I have no wish to condemn anyone before I discover the facts," he went on, quoting her own words and raising his voice as though she had not interrupted. "In a way, you are right. We do take things to extremes, and we should give other people the chance to explain themselves and their motives first."

"Do you really have to tell me all this?" she protested in embarrassment.

"Certainly I do. If it wasn't for you, it would never have entered my head. You accused me of arbitrary conduct and of banditry, and I don't want you to think of me like that."

"But, Signore—"

"Don't call me Signore," he snapped. "We're about the same age, aren't we? My name is Carlo." He shook his head, as though worrying about something, and added, half to himself, "I always thought 'Marion' when I thought of you."

"Oh, please listen to me."

"Yes, well, we mustn't go too quickly. For the moment we are talking about that woman, about Luciana's mother. I intend to give her a chance."

Marion bit her lip and wished, again, that she were anywhere else but here. "You must do as you wish," she said, "it isn't my affair."

"But it is, partly. It was you who made me think. You may be wrong, of course. She may be only a trollop in the end, or she may be trying to squeeze money out of us, but that is a risk I am prepared to take; she might be quite sincere. So I hired a lawyer."

"You what?"

"Yes," he proclaimed triumphantly, "a man who makes inquiries. And this lawyer of mine is inquiring about that protégée of yours, if I may call her so."

"But do remember, I've never met her, either."

"You took her part. That is enough. We have to find out what the truth is to prevent our being—arbitrary, wasn't it? —And to help us come to an agreement for the sake of justice, and for Luciana's sake. If we possibly can, of course."

"And you truly are doing this?"

"I am."

"Then that means—"

It meant that the whole thing was straightened out. Georgette Lassalle had nothing to do except, perhaps, mediate, and that would not be difficult now. There would be a reconciliation and Luciana had nothing to fear from either side. There would be no heartbreaks or cruel separations, but an amicable understanding to safeguard and protect her.

Marion was on the verge of telling him just how delighted she was, when it occurred to her that she could not do so without confessing the undercover role she had been playing in his house. No, she must leave Carlo to himself. The idea and the good intention were his and he should rightfully do it all and receive the thanks due to him.

She, meanwhile, would go back to Paris and explain that plans could be dropped, since there was to be a new agreement on a friendly basis, made with Luciana's best interests in mind. And how thankful she was to have done nothing to facilitate what Mlle Lassalle referred to as the rescue of "that poor child" from "that dreadful family."

"You're pleased?" Carlo had been studying the relieved, expressive face.

"So pleased. I do congratulate you. You're doing a very good thing, Carlo."

"Well, as to that, we have to wait and see what she's like first. We must be sure she's morally fit to be with Luciana; then we can start talking."

"If this is the Sardinian way, then I respect it. You are being fair and honorable, whatever happens, and I admire you for it."

She spoke warmly, with evident sincerity and as they reached the house he replied, "I am very glad to hear you say that."

Alma was pushing the wheelchair across the hall. As they entered her expression held more murder than welcome in it. Marion went up to continue packing and Carlo stayed chatting to his grandmother.

"LUCIANA! Has Luciana come home? Has anybody seen her?"

Francesca's terrified voice rang through the house and brought family and servants running. Doors banged open and shut as she and Giuseppe declaimed and shouted together and in turn.

"But she was with you. Where have you left her?" demanded the Marchesa.

"She went. They picked her up. We thought she had come home in the car."

"Car? What car?"

Now panic-stricken everyone gathered and questions poured in from all sides. Francesca regained her breath and tried to explain.

"It was black. A black car took her away."

"A car took her away? What were you thinking of to let her get in? And Giuseppe, didn't he stop them?" The Marchesa threw herself at the girl and shook her. Then an authoritative voice from above them cut through the hubbub.

"What the devil's going on down there?" Carlo, roused from his rest, had appeared at the top of the stairs. Clearly, something was very wrong. He came down the stairs two at a time. Almost immediately Marion followed, white as a sheet, and stood clinging to the bannister.

"It's Luciana. They let someone take her away." His mother's voice was anguished. She pointed at the sobbing Francesca and to Giuseppe, who was shaking and babbling unintelligibly.

"Let's hear what they have to say," ordered Carlo sternly. "Giuseppe, what are you talking about?"

With much gesticulation and stumbling over his words, the old man told his tale. Francesca went into a store, and Luciana followed her—

"Which store?"

"Where they sell baskets."

"And then? Be quick, we haven't got all day."

"I took the horse to the fountain, I never saw the little one come out of the shop. But then I saw her a bit farther along the street, talking to somebody, near a car."

"Who?"

"It was a lady."

"What sort of lady?"

"Oh, like a city lady. Like one of the tourists."

Carlo and his mother exchanged glances.

"There was another woman, too. She was driving."

Marion's heart gave a dizzy lurch and her head began to swim.

"And this woman—what did she look like?"

Giuseppe hadn't had time to see properly. "I was watching the lady talking to Luciana. The little one was making her laugh, I thought, the things she says. But I went into the shop to call Francesca to fetch her. In case she was annoying her, you know. And then—"

"Then what?" Carlo was barely keeping his anger under control.

"Francesca came out. And when I turned the car was driving away, and she wasn't there. Then we saw her, waving to us out of the back window. We ran after them." He struggled to continue. "They went around the corner and I unhitched the horse as fast as I could and we started off. We thought they must be coming here and we'd see the car coming this way. But they were going too fast, and we couldn't see them at all."

The Dowager Marchesa, who had listened in silence, intervened suddenly in the Sardinian dialect and Carlo nodded agreement.

"We'll notify the police." He spoke directly to Marion, as though no one else were concerned. She was still at the foot of the staircase, leaning against the bannister to save herself from falling. He could see the state she was in but misunderstood the cause.

"Don't worry," he added gently. "They're sure to find her."

"I doubt if she's as sure of that as you are!" came Alma's loud, malicious voice.

Carlo turned in her direction. "Why do you say that?"

"Because this has been planned for ages. She came and stood in front of Marion. "I never thought it would happen quite so soon. You didn't know, but I've been

watching you. And I'd have stopped you from leaving
with Luciana—I'd have put someone on your tail. But
they can manage without you, apparently. You've told
them all they need to know."

She gazed at Carlo, wringing her hands dramatically.
"I shall never forgive myself. Never!"

She was the center of alarmed attention, but Carlo
frowned and pulled her sharply away.

"What are you talking about? What do you think
you're doing? Have you taken leave of your senses?"

"Ask her!" was the triumphant reply.

Uncertainly, inquiringly, his eyes traveled from her
to Marion. There was silence, as though life itself hung
on what Alma would say next.

"Just look at her! If that isn't guilt, what is? She never
thought she'd be caught red-handed. She thought she'd
have time to make off before her gang got to work."

"Got to work?" echoed Donna Eleonora in
bewilderment.

"Before they kidnapped Luciana. Can't you
understand?"

"That's not true," Marion whispered but her pallor
and her trembling mouth belied her and Carlo did not
fail to observe them. His expression froze, as if whatever was coming next was too infamous to listen to.

"Explain yourself," he said to Alma, bleakly.

She took a paper from her jacket pocket and waved it
at him.

"There you are—that ought to enlighten you. I found
it in her room, hidden away in the desk. I was keeping
it to show you when you came back. Obviously I should
have let you know before."

Marion gasped. "You had no right to steal that; it
belongs to me."

"You see—she admits it!" Alma crowed.

While Carlo read she turned to the others, an eager
commentator. "That's the plan; the plan to kidnap Lu-

ciana. That's what our charming Mademoiselle came here for, to plan a kidnapping. What a viper she's been!"

This evoked exclamations of horror and Marion saw the faces around her change, grow alien and hostile. "It can't be true," said Donna Eleonora, staring at her, stunned. And in that moment Marion fought free of her paralysis, raised her head and confronted them.

"Yes," she said, "it is true. That plan was sent to me here, not long after I came; but I never wished to use it, so I left it in the drawer. And I swear that I have nothing to do with what has happened now. I swear it," she repeated earnestly.

She had spoken in French, but Alma was capable of retort in the same language.

"And who do you think's going to believe that? Aren't you ashamed to stand there and say such a thing?" For the benefit of the others she went on in Italian. "She was a spy, she was finding out how Luciana could be stolen; then she told her gang. Isn't it as clear as daylight? Luciana's mother sent her."

"Thank you, we can see she did." Carlo cut her short and spoke, his face impassive, to Marion. "That is a fact, is it not?"

She relinquished the bronze rail and answered him with a nod. Traces of color were returning to her lips.

"I thought I was doing the right thing, serving the cause of justice. But then I changed my mind." She was looking straight at him now. "When I had seen a little more and understood a little better, it seemed a dreadful idea. That's why I gave notice."

"Notice?" he repeated.

"Yes," put in his mother, "she gave notice. She was leaving the day after tomorrow."

"When everything was nicely over," Alma interposed. "What hypocrisy."

The Dowager Marchesa spoke in her gutteral, imperious voice. She ignored Marion throughout the conversation and addressed her daughter-in-law, who turned to Carlo.

"Mamma is right. We have a court order and this woman has broken the law in coming here with such a purpose. She will have to make a proper statement to the police."

"We must find Luciana before we do anything else," he answered.

"Of course you must, and I can help you!" cried Marion.

"You?" Donna Eleonora withered her with a look. "I thought you said you had nothing to do with it?"

"I think I can guess what's happened, though."

"No, we should go to the police immediately," repeated the Marchesa. "Carlo, you can tell them to watch the airports and the docks."

"But they'll be miles away before all that's organized," said Marion urgently. "Alert the police, yes, but you must do something else now!"

Carlo considered her words.

"They won't be leaving the island by any of the normal ways," he said.

"If her mother's taken her, then Luciana's name would have to be on her passport," Donna Eleonora agreed. "Still, it's easy enough to get hold of false documents, they say, if you descend to this sort of thing."

"Allow me to point out," her son replied, "that three years ago I descended to it myself. That woman is doing what we did, that's all. Don't let's waste time throwing stones."

"You're not defending her?" she exclaimed in a shocked voice.

"I am merely trying to be fair and objective. But that won't stop me from using every possible means to get Luciana back." He caught and held Marion's pleading gaze. "The truce is over," he said.

"But you must listen to me. There's been enough drama and violence already and Luciana will be the one to suffer if you insist on more. I've learned a great deal, living here with you. And I'm not a hypocrite, or a viper, or any of those things. Oh, it's hard for you to believe me, I know, but I've come to love your Luciana very much and her happiness depends on your listening.

"When I first came I was convinced that I would be rescuing a poor, mistreated child. I honestly thought you were just obstinate and feudal and she was being sacrificed to pride and prejudice. I hadn't realized how kind you were, nor how you loved and cherished her.

"But you must realize that her mother doesn't know that, yet. How could she? You would never meet Paulette or accept her. So of course she was determined to take back what you had stolen from her, even if she had to use force to do it. But what does force ever solve? There is another way."

"When I was the offending party," Carlo said, "there was another way. Not now. Now we have been offended and the situation is reversed. And it will be reversed again, I can assure you."

"Oh, this eternal pride of yours."

As though she had not spoken, he continued in the same peremptory tone, "After this morning's performance, any agreement is out of the question. There is nothing we can do."

"If I fetch Luciana back, without conditions, will you talk to her mother? Will you let her have her natural rights again and come to an arrangement that suits everyone, including Luciana?"

"Then you would be mixed up in it," Alma shouted. "Who's going to fall for that?"

"I don't want anybody to fall for anything." Only Carlo mattered, so Marion spoke to him alone. "I don't know what their exact plans are, but I think I know

where to find them before they leave the island. Once
they're gone it will be too late. Let me try. Lend me a
car."

"You wouldn't do any such crazy thing," Alma exploded. "Give her a car. You wouldn't see her for
smoke. She wants to dodge the police, that's all. She's
frightened to death."

Marion did not even hear her. "We have about three
hours, probably. If I don't telephone by then, you can
assume I was too late. And if you want to take any
steps against me, well, I'll be here."

"I'll bet. Do you seriously imagine you can get out of
it like that? Do you think we're all children or
something?"

"Let her go, Carlo. I have every faith in her."

Marion had not known the Dowager Marchesa spoke
French, but the unbelievable words she spoke were in
that language, despite the thick Sardinian accent.

"You won't regret it." She ran to the old lady's side.
"Luciana will come home with me and we'll see what
can be done for the future."

"Order the car and tell them to be quick about it,"
said Carlo's grandmother. And with an angry, "Basta!
Be quiet." she quelled Alma's almost incoherent
protests.

Carlo crossed to Marion. "Take the Alfa. Giuseppe
can drive you. Unless you'd like me to come with you?"

She shook her head and glanced hesitantly at the
Marchesa. "If your mother could come and wait in the
car when we get there, that might help."

"Me?" said Donna Eleonora, in some amazement. She
looked at her mother-in-law for direction, then to her
son and finally made up her mind.

"Why not? She's my granddaughter, and I'll do anything to have her back. Yes, I'll be ready in a minute."

The Marchesa dismissed the servants, then turned to
deal with her secretary. "I want to speak to you," she

said and Alma, boiling with impotent fury, followed her out of the room.

Carlo went to find the chauffeur and Marion had run upstairs to her bedroom. She was sure that Georgette Lassalle would be taking the child to France by plane. There was a plane from Olbia at seven o'clock—that must be the one. Everything depended on her. She prayed with all her heart she might succeed.

CHAPTER 14

Signora Petrucci was busy filling her best china coffee cups when the buzzer sounded from the door downstairs. She went to the hall and spoke into the microphone.

"Yes?"

It was a woman's voice. "I'd like to see Signore Petrucci, please."

"You can't, I'm afraid, he isn't here." There was an infinitesimal pause. "He's gone out."

"When can I see him? It's extremely urgent."

"This evening. Not before nine at the earliest."

And the plane goes at seven, Marion thought. *I was right.* That was a relief, at any rate.

"In that case, could I possibly see you, Signora? Now, I mean? We have met."

"Who is it?" The response was wary but interested.

"Marion Maraval. I'm a friend of Georgette Lassalle, in Paris."

"Oh, yes. Would you mind waiting, please?"

Signora Petrucci returned to the living room, her

husband and their guests. When she announced the name, Georgette Lassalle sat bolt upright.

"How did she know we were here?" she cried.

"Is anyone with her?" demanded her companion.

"I don't think so; though there might be, of course."

Paulette Arnaudy was the first to recover. She stood up, her face working.

"My God, they've found out. We must get away from here quickly!"

The other tried to allay her fears. "Now, wait. We can't be sure that she knows we're here, really. She's probably heard what's happened and she might have come to the Petruccis for shelter. Things can't be any too pleasant for her up at the castle just now. She was leaving the day after tomorrow in any case. Maybe she decided to go sooner, that's all."

"I wouldn't be surprised," Signore Petrucci agreed.

"She wants to see you," his wife told him. "She says it's urgent."

"Well, I'd better see her, then. Show her into the office," he replied.

Georgette Lassalle shook her head. "No, I'll see her. She obviously knows we've taken Luciana. I hadn't told her what the actual plans were, but she'll have put two and two together."

"Why did she let us down like that?" Paulette was bitter.

"She's entitled to scruples, and she developed them. But I know her, I think. She wouldn't give us away."

"You see her if you want to," said Paulette unwillingly, "I certainly won't. And do get rid of her as soon as you can. Lucy's fast asleep, so she won't make a sound. This Marion Maraval needn't know that she and I are here at all."

"If you go into the next room," suggested Signora Petrucci, "you could hear what she says."

"I don't particularly want to, thank you."

"Well," said Lassalle, "she is my client when all's
said and done, and I suppose I ought to know what she
wants. Will you ask her to come up, please?"

"She'll be getting impatient by now." The hostess
disappeared and a moment later Marion found herself
face to face with Georgette at the door of the now-
empty room. Keenly aware that time was running
short, she went straight to the point and explained just
why she had backed out of the assignment.

"And I'm absolutely sure," she concluded fervently,
"that the main, basic trouble is this huge misunderstanding between the two sides. Violence won't settle
anything."

"But heavens, they're the violent ones," was the rejoinder. "All we've done is borrow their own methods.
How else do you suggest we get the child back when a
judge has awarded custody to the mother and the father's family won't accept the ruling?"

"You're forgetting, custody was awarded to them,
too, by a judge in Sardinia. His is the ruling they
accept."

"Then it's an impasse. The only way out is to do
exactly as they did. That's fair, isn't it?"

"No, because it's no way out. Violence only leads to
more violence. If you manage to get Luciana off the
island—and I don't know that you will, because they're
watching all the exits—"

"If not today, then another day," said Georgette,
unmoved. "Nothing in this world will stop her mother
getting her back."

"But she's going to miss her father's family. People
she loves. And they love her, you know. They adore
her."

"A mother's rights are sacred; they come first."

"No mother can want to see her child suffering the
effects of quarrels and disputes she doesn't
understand."

"A five-year-old gets over things quite quickly."

"But think what scars a separation like that must leave. You snatch her away from all the tenderness and care she's used to, and you put her down in strange surroundings—"

Before she could finish speaking the door flew open and Paulette Arnaudy burst into the room, face contorted, black eyes blazing, and attacked her like a fury.

"You believe every word they say. You're on their side."

Marlon had recoiled involuntarily from this onslaught and the Lady Detective, as best she could, made hasty introductions. She mentioned how kindly Marion had agreed to substitute for Florence Montagne, and how very helpful she had been. The other calmed down and apologized.

"I'm sorry," she said, "you'll have to forgive me. I'm terribly upset, I'm afraid, but all this is so important to me. It's been a ghastly three years, waiting to get Lucy back, and I still can't believe she's really here. And there is nothing, nothing, I wouldn't do to keep her now."

"Is she all right?"

"She's asleep. She was tired after the ride."

But Marion was not entirely happy about that ride. "Did she mind coming with you? She wasn't frightened, or anything?"

"She didn't know me." Paulette was trying not to cry and the recollection obviously rankled. "We told her we were friends, and she liked the drive in the car, but when we got here she began to feel lost. She wanted her grandmother and her uncle, and someone called Francesca. She wanted you, as well. Oh, God. Think of having your own child looking at you as though you were a stranger. She was afraid. Think what that's like, if you can. That's what they've done, your precious Terralbas." She dabbed at her eyes, angrily. "What can they ever, ever do to make amends? I detest them, loathe them all!"

Hatred and despair twisted her handsome features out of recognition, but the famous voice was still the same—the voice that had lured Eficio away from home and country and the tradition of his race.

"The man you loved was a Terralba, though," Marion reminded her gently.

"He was different, quite different!" cried Paulette forcibly. "He may not have had all those antique virtues, but at least his heart wasn't made of stone."

"Their hearts are not stone, either, I assure you."

"Now they've turned you into a Terralba too. How did they manage that, I wonder? Did you come here simply to tell me how marvelous they are?"

"I came here for Luciana's sake and for no other reason."

"Lucy, her name's Lucy," was the irate rejoinder.

"Lucy, Luciana, what does it matter? You all love her just the same, don't you?"

"My God, you're not by any chance comparing the love of her own mother with their ... their pride? It's pride and revenge with that breed, and nothing else. It always has been."

But Marion was determined to convince her. She knew what she wanted to say and the words came with a rush.

"You spoke of mother love just now. Well, there's your husband's mother too, remember; she's had exactly the same thing to go through. She and you lost the same person. Once he went away, she never saw Eficio again. Isn't it natural that all her affection goes to your daughter? Luciana is his child."

This seemed to make an impression. Paulette did not reply at once, but gradually the anger faded from her face.

"That's no reason to take her away from me," she said at last, reluctantly.

Too perceptive to interfere, Georgette Lassalle sat by in silence. As soon as Marion began to speak she had known the interview would have results, despite its bad beginning. Marion, indeed, surprised her, for she seemed altogether more mature and resolute. This was not the young woman who had wept in her apartment a few months earlier; escaping, coming abroad and living with this family had changed her entirely. And Georgette also wondered, hearing the burning conviction of her arguments, what else her client had discovered that she had lacked before.

"Why don't you both sit down?" she said.

"It's getting late," Marion pointed out.

"It's getting late for us, as well. We must be leaving soon." Then Paulette flared at Marion again. "Whose side are you on? And have you told them where we are?"

"No, of course I haven't. I hope you don't think I would do any such thing."

"No. No, I suppose not." The concession was made unwillingly, but the beautiful, ravaged face relaxed a little.

"Thank you,"

Georgette Lassalle recognized her moment, stirred in the armchair and put out her cigarette. "I presume you had some definite purpose in coming here," she said. "What do you suggest?"

"Peace."

"Peace? With those people?" Paulette started up again. "When they've treated me like a kitchenmaid; when they've tricked and humiliated me? Because I happened to marry their son and acquire their name, they're like sworn enemies. Well, I'll show them how much their name means to me. It's on my legal papers, and that's all."

"But it's your daughter's name, too. You can't change that."

"And what does that matter, I'd like to know? It's only a name, and she'll have nothing else from the Terralbas. If she's as proud as I am, she won't even want to speak to them when she grows up and sees what they've done to me."

"At this age, though, she loves them dearly. She's going to miss them more than you imagine."

"She'll get over it."

"But she's had their warmth and love for three years—she's been settled for three years. How will you make up for that?"

"I shall be there," said Paulette.

"No theater? No films? No singing? Are you retiring, then?"

"Of course I'm not retiring. That's my life; it's what I live for. No, I shall take her with me, everywhere. An actess can be a good mother, for heaven's sake. I won't be the first."

"Oh, but you've seen those children," protested Marion. "You know what it does to them. Dragged about all over the place and never the same person looking after them in each city. I don't think that's a good idea. And what about her schooling?"

"Oh? And what would you advise, may I ask?" enquired Paulette with heavy sarcasm.

"Leave her at Castel Terralba and see her when you have the time to devote to her."

"Leave her? With them? To be brought up hating me? I can hear it now. 'That dreadful woman, your mother.' No!"

"But they love her. And nobody has ever said a word against you to her there, I'm sure of that."

"Oh, no. They've told her that I'm dead."

"They said nothing. I told her you were in heaven," Marion corrected her

"It comes to the same thing, doesn't it?"

"No, it leaves a kind of loophole, don't you see? A star shines in heaven, and you're a star. Lucy wouldn't argue about that."

Paulette shrugged her shoulders impatiently, but she was wavering and looked questioningly at Georgette Lassalle, who still sat there, saying nothing. The fact was that Luciana had been pathetically frightened when she arrived with unknown people in an unknown house. And her mother was both disturbed and angry at the tears and demands to be taken home. Marion's reasoning had done nothing to restore her confidence; it worried her more than she cared to admit and had blunted the edge of victory.

Luciana had been not quite two when Carlo de Terralba snatched her from her nursemaid. Her life in their simpler and more personal atmosphere had no ill effects. In those days, with rehearsals, recording sessions, fittings, Paulette had had so little time to spare. And these days, what time was there? She was still racing between the fitting room, rehearsals and studios. If she took this sensitive small creature now, how could she compensate for, or ever make her forget, her baby years at Terralba?

Marion put her hand out.

"Why not draw a line through everything and start again. Let them get to know you. They are Luciana's family, after all, and Eficio's. They have an image of you concocted out of odds and ends of prejudice and gossip; they have no idea that you are kind, or generous, or likeable. Let them see you as you really are, and you'll find out things can be settled."

"Thank you very much." Paulette ignored the proffered hand. "You may believe these flattering things about me, but in their view I'm a low woman who shouldn't be allowed across the doorstep."

"But you're so wrong! Listen. Luciana can't begin to

understand any of this, and she mustn't be upset by it. If you let her go back, for the time being, anyway, I give you my word that a friendly arrangement can be worked out. Then you'll all be happy and it will be so much better for her."

"Give Lucy back to them? I'd have to be out of my mind! When we've just risked everything in this cloak-and-dagger operation?" Enraged, she turned to Georgette Lassalle. "You hear this ... this appalling proposal?"

"And I think it's worth discussing," was the cool reply.

The color rushed to Paulette's cheeks. "Not you as well? Not now? When we've finally spirited her away, under their very noses?"

Georgette Lassalle placed another cigarette on the rim of the ashtray and shook her head.

"We're not out of the woods yet, you know. The opposition has a lot of influence, and it's their home ground. You heard what Marion said just now—they are guarding the docks and airports. The police are fairly slow as a rule and I was banking on our leaving before anything could be done, but however slow they are, there still isn't a plane before seven o'clock. I have hiding places ready, too, if we need them, but we are on an island, remember, and once the hunt is organized we're in a tough spot. It won't be all that easy to slip through an organized net. By ourselves, yes, but a small child makes it difficult."

"I thought you had everything arranged," said Paulette in a desolate voice.

"With Marion to help we should have had a longer start and time on our side. The picture changed when her help was withdrawn, but you didn't want to postpone the attempt, and I didn't blame you. Then Lucy herself is a problem: you saw how she reacted. Things just have not gone as smoothly as I'd hoped, and I really do wonder whether you might not be wise—"

"The hell with being wise. I will not go bleating to these people like a sheep to the slaughter. An eye for an eye."

"But do realize that you're not the only one involved," cried Marion hotly. "Can't you think about your daughter, instead of merely hating the Terralbas all the time?"

To this Paulette could say nothing but, "They'll have to make the first move, then."

"They already have."

"They have? What are you talking about?"

"Your mother-in-law, the Marchesa. She has taken the first step. She's willing to meet you, to discuss Luciana and come to some arrangement. And I think it might do a great deal of good."

"See me? When? Where?"

"Here," said Marion. "Now."

"The Marchesa—you've brought her here?" All Paulette's terror and indignation returned, and even Georgette frowned.

"Oh, not here, don't worry. I left her up at the Solitudine and didn't say where I was going. If you agree to talk, you'll have to take Luciana with you and work something out with her there. And I'm sure you can."

"Take Lucy!"

"Listen. This reconciliation has been on my mind for some time. As soon as I met the Terralbas I knew that it was possible. I could see you had so little, if anything, to quarrel about. Nobody can judge what he doesn't know, and the whole affair's been a maze of misunderstandings. What they chiefly hate is the broken engagement, the fact that Eficio went back on his word. But it was his doing, not yours, and they can't hold you responsible. That's what I've been trying to explain to the present Marchese, and he's the fieriest and most unreasonable of them all."

"Carlo? That bandit, that gangster!"

"He's nothing of the kind," Marion retorted. "He's a Sardinian. They're savage and passionate, and so is he. Primitive if you like, but he is just and he is honorable. He listened to me when I reasoned with him. What's more, he was quite ready to apologize if he was mistaken about you."

A speculative gaze from the armchair dwelt on Marion. What a strong speech on behalf of the "bandit"....

"Why are you sticking up for him like this?" inquired Paulette suspiciously.

"I sincerely wanted to help—and it wasn't for the sake of the job, as Mademoiselle Lassalle will tell you. I was bitterly unhappy myself and I felt for you; and I must admit, I thought something interesting and different would take my mind off my own troubles. So I came here. But it wasn't in the least what I expected and I saw that you could come to terms without doing anything drastic. I learned to appreciate the Terralbas.

"I thought at first as you did—that they were gangsters, taking what they wanted and paying no attention to law and order. But truly, they are not like that at all. They are fine, straightforward people, and living with them is good for Lucy. If only you can give them a chance to know you properly they'll welcome you as her mother, and their sister. But you have to decide for yourself what to do."

Marion spoke with heart and soul and Paulette heard her out. One after another, the changing emotions were reflected in her face. Now the hardness melted away and this time it was she who extended her hand.

"You're right, and I should thank you for everything you've done. I'll wake Lucy up and we can go to the

Solitudine together. Georgette, will you drive me there?"

"With pleasure," said the Lady Detective.

Marion smiled at Luciana's mother. "It's the best thing you could do," she said. "I know it is."

She had talked with Eleonora during the long drive into Núoro and convinced her at last that, for the sake of the child, the old disputes must be forgotten. Paulette was the wife Eficio had chosen; her marriage had brought her into the family and as his widow her conduct had been exemplary. Her profession was slightly out of the ordinary, perhaps, but there was no stigma attached to it and she pursued it with talent and success. In a world eager for theatrical scandal her reputation was untouched, and no one had ever heard of her having a lover.

And if she and her husband had been foolish and extravagant, well, they were young and he might have had that consuming appetite for life that often exists in those who are doomed to an early death. Surely his mother could understand this, and forgive? The Marchesa, whose one fear was that she might lose Luciana, had listened and agreed.

"If she brings that child home, then all our doors are open to her. She can take her place among us with my blessing."

And that was that.

Paulette went to rouse her daughter, sleeping while these negotiations proceeded over her unconscious head, and Georgette Lassalle turned to her other client, laughing.

'Congratulations," she said. "I never realized you were such a diplomat. Are you coming with us for the next stage?"

Marion gave her directions for reaching the Solitudine but said, no, she would not come.

"Oh, well. Where are you going, then, if you don't mind my asking?"

"Why should I? I shall find a taxi, and go to Olbia and take the plane."

"The one we'll be catching?"

"I doubt whether we'll have Paulette Arnaudy with us. I rather imagine the Marchesa will persuade her to go home with her to the castle; she'll want to introduce her to them all and end the day with a general reconciliation."

"But you," Georgette repeated. "Why don't you go back with them?"

"I'm going to France," said Marion, and offered no further explanations.

"Oh. But did you bring your luggage?"

"No."

"But—"

"It's all packed and ready. I shall wire and they can send it on."

"If you intended to leave, why didn't you bring your luggage?"

"I didn't know how things would turn out. If Paulette had refused to take Luciana back they would have held me responsible for the kidnapping. I didn't want them to think I might be running away."

"It wasn't a kidnapping. She is the mother, when all is said and done."

"But I'm afraid I was still the spy who had abused the trust and hospitality of decent people."

"Good Lord, they wouldn't have cut your head off!"

"They would have despised me, which is quite as bad. And I should certainly have gone back. I promised."

"But I don't see why you have to disappear like this; practically slinking away when you're the one who straightened the whole thing out."

"I prefer to."

Marion averted her head and there was a tiny pause.

"I suppose this isn't the time or the place to discuss your own affairs?"

"I'd much rather wait until we reach Paris, if you don't mind."

"Well, I have a lot to tell you."

"Is the house . . . empty?" Marion inquired, in a carefully neutral voice.

The other nodded. "Maresco didn't even wait to be evicted. He won't trouble you again. Everything's under control; a few legal formalities, and you're absolutely free."

She pulled on her gloves. Steps were heard outside, and Marion could hear Luciana asking questions.

"Right," said Lassalle "no more problems here. All tidied up, I think."

"Yes," said Marion, "all tidied up."

And she thought of the long, long loneliness ahead.

CHAPTER 15

Marion felt like a stranger pacing the house; this house where she had planned to live in love and happiness and where she had discovered her love for what it was. She had regained her freedom, but the memory of the cruel revelation would not fade.

Many of the worst problems of Stanni's fraudulent intrusion into her life had been sorted out in her absence. The civil marriage had no legal existence, the religious marriage was in the process of annulment. Georgette Lassalle and M. Perdrière had managed to have the case heard privately, with none of the cheap and unpleasant publicity that Marion, who valued her peace and dignity, had dreaded.

In return for their signed statements, Maresco and his sister were allowed to vanish before they could be called to account. With this document safe in her possession, Georgette had cheated the newshounds of a sensational lawsuit and let him go. Everything, in fact, had passed off as quietly and smoothly as possible.

Only the bitter taste of wormwood and the wounds to heart and pride remained.

And this house, snuggled in among the carefully tended rock gardens, walled in for privacy, almost overgrown with ivy on one side and burgeoning with lily of the valley and bleeding hearts on the other—this former love nest remained as well. All the furnishing that she and Stanni had picked out together had been immediately put up for sale, including the wall hanging that a very dear friend had given them for their first wedding anniversary. Marion didn't want any trace of Stanni's presence to remain in the house, while she decided whether or not to sell it.

Preoccupied, Marion strolled through the living room. Stripped of sofa, chairs, carpeting and drapes, it still retained something bitter. If she listened hard, Marion could almost hear the tinkling and clinking of a glass being filled with ice cubes. With a start, she turned, but the table that had held the tray of cocktail glasses and decanters was gone, along with everything else. She sighed. He haunted this place. She would have to sell it.

Theresa, the girl from the villa at l'Oursinade, had arrived several days earlier, and was busily packing away china and books into huge cartons destined to go into storage until such a time as the wounds had healed. Fondly, Marion gazed at the carved cuckoo clock from the Black Forest, the "graduation" gift from a friend of her late father, even though Félicien's death had cut short her schooling. Stanni had hated that clock. He had tolerated its presence on the wall only if it weren't running. Guests to the house who noticed the clock and inquired about it were told that it was "right twice a day."

Marion went over to the wall and took the clock down. She would pack it with those items that didn't remind her of Stanni and treasure it for the good memories it aroused in her. At the sound of footsteps Theresa looked up from her work. A sturdy, ruddy-cheeked farm girl, she had the steadiness and cheerfulness of temperament that Marion had always associated with the countryside around l'Oursinade. Now, the two women looked at each other and smiled.

"Are you sorry to be moving, Madame?" asked Theresa, who, from the moment of her arrival, had been visibly impressed with the interior of the house.

"I don't know," sighed Marion, "I just don't know, Theresa."

Marion was genuinely wondering what her next move was to be. She could have gone to live at l'Oursinade, but she had always thought of the summer house as a retreat. The Marion who had stood up so eloquently to Paulette Arnaudy, who had defended Paulette against the baseless accusations of the Terralba family, who had literally gone to do battle for the protection of Lucy-Luciana Terralba, was not about to take refuge in a summer house for the rest of her life, or even for the rest of the week.

The Marion who had existed before could never have broken ties with this quaint little home in Saint-Cloud, as this Marion was now so ruthlessly doing. She packed the few treasures that would accompany her to her next home, wherever that might be—the cuckoo clock, the music box her father had given her for her fourteenth birthday, her school books, autographed by her favorite teachers. Oh, certainly they were all sentimental souvenirs, but Marion had discovered that sentiment was nothing to be afraid of. During the two years with Stanni, she had forbade herself the display of too much sentiment, since it seemed to embarrass him, without realizing that such restraint was slowly bending her out of shape and turning her into the kind of person who shrank from feelings. But those months at Castel Terralba with the emotional conflicts she had met and conquered there had restored her mental balance.

Castel Terralba. From time to time the walls of the castle would come into her mind, along with the image of a tall, striding, dark-haired man with laughing eyes . . . who thought she had betrayed him.

At last, she understood what Alma had seen in Carlo, even though in the time Marion was there, she had never seen him breaking in a horse. Amid the fiery passions, the argumentativeness, the stubbornness, he offered something that Marion had been looking for and had sacrificed for the happiness of a five-year-old girl. In Carlo there was the promise of comfort, of security. His single-minded devotion to duty included the kind of selfless love that any woman would be glad to receive, including Marion. How, then, oh, how had they wound up adversaries?

The question was rhetorical—the past was past, and her ties with the Terralbas cut, as surely as her ties to Stanni had been severed. And yet, something had begun to grow in her at the castle, something that Carlo nourished with his talk about archeology, bandits, vendettas. This something had taken solid root in her heart, and she could feel it move inside her at the thought of those white walls and those turrets standing out against the unbelievable blue of the sky.

At times, in a daydream, she would find herself wondering what her life would have been like if Paulette Arnaudy had never entered it, if she had taken the job as governess with no strings attached and was still living in the castle. At those times, the something in her heart wrenched painfully, and she forced her thoughts onto another track. It was better not to dwell on some memories. Carlo was a closed chapter of her life; in time, she would be able to forget him. She was young, there would be other men.

But no other Carlo.

Almost angrily, Marion shook her head to clear it of these thoughts.

"I'll be in the studio upstairs, Theresa."

"Very good, Madame," said Theresa, watching Marion's progress out the living-room door and into the corridor.

The studio, that infamous room where Marion had first heard the unwitting confession of her husband, was stripped almost as bare as the rest of the house. What furniture had not actually been sold was in storage, awaiting a buyer. Marion glanced through the tall, narrow windows into her garden. If only the yard were covered with snow! England had had such lovely snow. What a miserable climate Paris had— unbearably hot and humid in summer, cool and drizzly in spring and autumn and cold and dry in the winter.

Paradoxically, the garden was the only part of the house that Marion truly regretted leaving, even though it justified this feeling for only three months of the year; the rest of the time it was too soggy or too barren to be enjoyed. At this time of the year, the fruit trees extended supplicating branches, blackened and brittle, toward her, and the limp brown stems of the peonies and lilies lay like straws against the dark soil of the flower beds.

Sighing, Marion tore herself away from the windows and fell wearily into the last remaining chair in the room. Except for the multitude of doors in the place, this room could have been the stage setting for the play by Sartre, called *Huis Clos*—naked walls, stripped floor and windows and a single piece of furniture, exactly as specified in the stage directions. There was a copy of the play in her book box; she would have to reread it. It was about three characters who have died and are on their way to hell; but they pause for a while in limbo to compare notes on their lives.

How appropriate, she thought, considering what she

had recently been throngh! And what a perfectly apt place for her to sit and contemplate on the past few years! She would have laughed, if the urge to cry had not overtaken her first.

Suddenly, the bell rang at the garden entrance, and Theresa went to answer it

"If it's the carpenter or anyone like that, bring him up," Marion called. "Otherwise, I'm out."

She could hear the girl arguing, then a brisk step sounded in the corridor and a rippling, resonant voice echoed in the hall to the studio where she was sitting.

"It is someone like that; I'm here with the luggage, anyhow! May I come in?" Paulette Arnaudy's famous laugh accompanied the words.

Marion jumped to her feet. "Heavens, I didn't mean you!" she exclaimed. "How lovely to see you."

Paulette hugged her. "Well, you deserter, how are you?"

"Deserter? Me?"

"A dreadful deserter. Running away like that, when I needed you to introduce me to my terrifying relatives."

Marion took Paulette's leopard-skin coat, cleared a pile of clothes from one of the few remaining chairs and seated her visitor.

"Do forgive all this. I'm in the midst of moving."

Paulette disposed her slim form among the cushions and waves of Dior scent wafted around her.

"You just got back now?" Marion inquired.

"This morning. Think of it—I go for a day and I'm there for a month!"

"And how was it?"

"Couldn't have been better." The dark eyes danced, but it was with a catch in her voice that she continued. "You were right, my dear; they grow on you, those Ter ralbas. When I got to know her, my mother-in-law turned out to be a lamb—once she decided to take me as she found me, that is. And la mamma—my goodness, what a woman! And what a part, if you put her in a play! And then Maria Pia—'' she waved her long, shapely hands and laughed again, ''—I taught Maria Pia how to dance to rock music. We're friends for life.'' She glowed with infectious youth and happiness; it was a joy to be with her.

''They really are sweet, though,'' she went on more seriously, ''and I felt I knew them by the time we got there. Donna Eleonora told me so much about them on the way. Once she had her granddaughter safely on her knee she was quite ready to help me all she could. And that place!''

''And how is Luciana getting on?''

Paulette's face lit up with maternal pride.

''Living like a queen with a lot of devoted slaves. They all revolve round her, from the old lady down to the odd-job man.'' She sighed. ''So what could I do against a whole little world like that? And she is so perfectly happy with them.''

''You'll let her stay there, then?''

''Yes. I'm going off on tour soon and it's better to leave her where she is than drag her round the country.''

She stopped to think, as though genuinely surprised at what she had just said. ''I never would have believed I could give in so easily and do exactly what they wanted! I missed her so. But when I thought it over, well, you were right. They can do such a lot for her, give her more of a childhood, more security, than I can. For the time being, at any rate,'' she added wistfully.

''But you'll see her often,'' Marion said, to comfort her.

''Whenever I can. Oh, my goodness, why don't I retire? I must be mad. But I think her father would have liked to see her growing up in his old home, with his mother and his grandmother. After he destroyed their peace and all their hopes, because of me, I think he would have been comforted by the outcome. In this life," she said, "you have to pay for things."

Neither spoke for a moment and Marion wrestled with a ridiculous desire to cry.

"You've acted in the child's best interests," she said at last. "She'll appreciate that later on."

"Well," said Paulette briskly, to suppress her own emotions, "let's leave that for now. Let's talk about the gangster."

"What gangster?"

"You know, my brother-in-law, the pirate who kidnapped my child." She laughed. "We buried the hatchet, Carlo and I, and he really is the nicest creature, except, of course, he will go on about his old stone images and his beloved archeology. It's all he ever thinks about. Oh, and that reminds me—your suitcases."

"Suitcases?" The connection seemed obscure.

"I told you, I brought them with me. They're downstairs, I'll have them brought up for you."

"Oh, please, you mustn't—"

"No trouble, the chauffeur can carry them," and Paulette was gone.

Marion pursued her uselessly to the top of the steps. "Do leave them. Theresa and I can manage."

"No, they weigh a ton. The chauffeur's pretty hefty."

Marion smiled and let her go. In Paulette she recognized herself as she used to be—impulsive, spontaneous, dashing at things. Then she heard a heavy tread and went to take her bags from the man, who deposited them on the floor with an exaggerated groan.

"What on earth have you got in there?" he demanded. "Solid gold bullion or a colossus from Sassari?"

Her cheeks flushed and her heart began to thump. Carlo.

"But what are you doing, hauling up my luggage?"

"Somebody has to haul it up, I suppose." He sank into a chair with every appearance of exhaustion, only to leap from it immediately and stand straight and tall, looking down at her. She had never seen him in ordinary winter clothes before; the wind had ruffled his hair a little.

"Incidentally, good morning."

"Good morning." She still could not believe that he was there.

"Is that all? Good morning, Carlo."

"Good morning, Carlo."

"Marion." He bent toward her, put his hands on her shoulders and kissed her twice, fiercely, pressing her to him. When he let her go she was shaken and confused, uncertain whether to laugh or cry.

"Don't look so taken aback." he said. "People do that all the time, when they meet at stations."

"But we're not at a station," she said weakly.

"We're not?" Doubtfully he inspected the room. "There's no furniture; there's no carpet. you haven't any pictures on the wall."

"I'm moving."

"Are you, indeed?"

He digested this information. Watching the reflective, strong-willed face she acknowledged to herself that he had come to occupy an inconceivably important place in her life. This man she had known so short a time, this hostile, provoking person, with his infuriating notions—he still made her feel secure and happy as soon as he walked in. She felt something deeper, too, that she refused to analyse.

A station waiting room was exactly what the house resembled, exactly what it was. And in that instant it became that and nothing more. The last traces of bitterness and resentment vanished; the time she had spent here was suddenly a detached episode from someone else's life. The weight of it rolled away and she was

entirely, truly free, although so many things must yet
be decided. All at once she realized that they were still
standing, face to face, in silence, and wanted to laugh.

"We're like a couple of graven images. Couldn't we
sit down?"

"Not until you tell me what made you leave the island like that, as if you had the whole police force after
you. They hadn't even started."

He was joking, but she was up in arms directly.

"How do you imagine I felt? What must you have
thought when you discovered I was spying?"

"I was waiting for you to explain," he replied calmly,
though she had thrown the word at him as if it were
contaminated. "That's what you should have done.
You owed it to me. To both of us, that is." His eyes, and
the way he spoke, forbade her to misunderstand his
meaning.

"You had Alma there, why didn't she explain? She'd
taken that paper, she could have produced some marvelous motives for it all."

"Leave Alma out of this. She left when Paulette arrived—and that was thanks to you." The coaxing note
came into his voice again. "So why not tell me properly? To begin with, I'd like to know how that woman
lawyer ever acquired an assistant like you. And how
could you possibly plunge in as you did, without
knowing the first thing about anyone concerned? It
isn't like you."

So he had been to see Georgette Lassalle.

"She didn't tell you?"

"You are forgetting professional secrecy. No, Mademoiselle Lassalle is hardly lacking in courage and goes
quite as near the limits of the law as I did, let me say,
but she stood firm on professional secrecy. Your address was all we could get out of her. And she only gave
us that," he added severely, "because we had to deliver
the suitcases." Amiable but determined, he pushed her

into an armchair and took the chair beside her. "Couldn't you tell me? Tell me what it is you're worrying about."

Her hand was still in his. She withdrew it and pushed a stray lock from her forehead. "It's a long story, I warn you," she sighed.

"Never mind, I can listen, can't I? I'm a friend, you know that."

A friend. Their eyes met. Yes, almost from the first time she had seen him, she had known it; before she even knew who he was. And known it beyond a doubt since she ran so far away from him. He had come after her and the burden of loneliness was gone as if a miracle had spirited it away.

Some time later, Paulette Arnaudy tapped at the door. She had heard the monologue go on and on, tiptoed upstairs twice already and tiptoed tactfully down. But silence had fallen at length; all should be over. She made a cautious inspection before entering the room. Marion's head lay on Carlo's shoulder and he was caressing her hair.

"I'd hate to miss the happy ending. May I come in?"

As though emerging from a dream, Marion stood up hastily. Miles away again—what was she dreaming of?

"I've walked all around the garden, more than once, every corner of it. I've helped that little shepherdess of yours to pack some china and we managed to break two cups and a saucer, I fear. You must have settled something by now. Another kidnapping, by any chance?"

"You could call it that," Carlo agreed. "An abduction, perhaps. I have decided to make away with Marion, but I don't think she minds."

"You're rushing things," Marion protested. "I didn't say—"

"Oh, he'll always rush things. Once a pirate, always a pirate. You'll never change him. Never."

"I'd never want to!" As on another occasion, the words slipped out.

"That's what I like to hear," said Paulette, in tones of hearty approval. "Now, what do we do with the suitcases?"

"Take them away again," said Carlo, without hesitation.

"Hold it a minute," exclaimed Marion, "Let me have a moment to breathe! Besides, I have to think about—"

"Think about what? Everything's arranged." He turned to Paulette. "She's coming back to Sardinia. Isn't it fortunate, she absolutely adores that village of mine on the road to Sassari — a most unusual *nuraghe*, and it's going to produce some interesting finds. Well, she says she's thought of nothing else ever since she left us, and she'll act as my assistant. Just a small formality first, in the chapel at Castel Terralba."

"We're going to be sisters-in-law!" Paulette was jubilant. "And can you imagine, Luciana will be your niece!"

"I'll love her even more than I do already."

Marion smiled across at Carlo as Paulette embraced her. A man she trusted; sure and solid, someone who would drive the past away. With him she would forget its wretchedness and keep only l'Oursinade, where Maresco had been nothing but an occasional visitor and there were no associations with the nightmare. It was a place Carlo would love.

But it was not l'Oursinade that she was seeing now. It was a white village around a medieval fortress, where people with proud, rugged faces walked through its narrow lanes and alleyways, a village cool in black shadows, blazing in the sun. That would be her country; that would be her life. She longed with all her heart to be there.

She had never expected to know happiness again. Now she recognized it, and it was due to this man, who looked so obstinate and was so kind—Carlo loved her. As hope and joy came flooding over her, the deep voice said, "Marion, you're miles away. What are you thinking about?"

She ran to him. "Us," she said. "I'm thinking about us."

What readers say about Mystique Books...

"You can't put them down once you start reading them."
— Mrs. H.M.,* Marion, Wisconsin

"I like them."
— J.K., Indianapolis, Indiana

"Undoubtedly the best novels I have ever read."
— D.M., Brooklyn, Michigan

"They're great. All characters are mature, sympathetic. Really readable."
— Mrs. W.L.T., Jacksonville, Florida

*Names available on request.